Age 14 and above

Copyright (c) 2014. Tn Odu. Nigeria's Phantom Publisher.

Published by Phantom House Books, Nigeria

118 Obafemi Awolowo Way, Ikeja

Lagos Nigeria 999999

in conjunction with Amazon Createspace PoD,

7290 B. Investment Drive, Charleston, SC 29418, Copyright © 2000 -

2011, CreateSpace, a DBA of On-Demand Publishing,

ISBN-10: 978-51078-1-7

ISBN-13: 978-978-51078-1-4

www.phantomhouseafrica.co.nr

[international dialing code:] 23481 3954 0895

The human race was no longer the human race. Times had changed. People had changed. Power had changed hands. We were nothing now, but relics of a past life. We'd spent too long squabbling…
Evolution had simply moved on.

haku & hrth

SURROGATE REALITY

persephone

Imagine a world with possibilities. Only for it no longer to exist. Not for them, anyway—the streets of Warri too cruel a place to grow up without a father—or some sort of mentor. They'd killed him, the loutish hooligans! Murdered in cold blood as he lay there by the street corner, lifeless in a grimy ditch—more blood oozing from the back of his head than the nasty gash he'd sustained from crashing through the windshield. "Palpa!" the boy sobbed, his beady brown pupils glazed by tears.

"Papa!!!" he shrieked in a bloodcurdling screech as passersby stood by. It'd been an accident, but who was to explain it to the poor boys? Damned hooligans. Filthy morons.

The late teen, Tagho, didn't look like one for tears—a fire in the boy's eye impossible to quench. His blood boiled over so he bolted for the end of the car and unhooked its trunk. Next minute, he was hurling a monkey wrench at one of the thugs responsible for all this. Yet, despite what they'd caused, their reaction to the monkey wrench wasn't kind. These were the streets of Warri, future capital of the Federal Republic of Every Man for Himself. The thugs went buck-wild and burst in a tantrum. One of them went as far as forming a fist with a thick neck towel, shamelessly smashing in the window of the now defunct Honda to pry out whatever stabbing instrument he could use to threaten the boys. His comrades, on the other hand, hailed curses from gods unseen. Even so, the older one didn't care. Not for the charade or the sharp objects coming his way. Their father lay dead in an unfinished gutter! It was his intent to send someone en suite. But in the end, the scuffle was brief and there was nothing the thronging crowds could do but watch the ebony teenager alongside any who dared interfere get the wind knocked out of them.

The thugs opted not to stab either of the teenagers for one death was enough already. Besides, a police van wasn't always far away from public disturbances like this one. It'd be hard to explain to DSPC the unlawful extortion of local commuter buses. Or this accident.

Who knew interrupting traffic could cause a man to take a wild turn and swing for the left? Still, it wasn't their fault the old fruit had unhinged his seatbelt for a piss earlier. Or failed to pay for necessary repairs to fix a faulty car door? or the phone call he was said to have been making.

An armoured vehicle veered into sight and the scoundrels took off. "Tagho! They are running, Tagho!" Ruke yelped, abandoning his father's corpse to aid his elder brother in pursuing the alleged killers. Sadly the thugs divided their run to bewilder the single police unit, but the brothers couldn't separate themselves lest they be swallowed whole by the city's pervading beehive of bustle and activity. So much to their chagrin, the teenagers let the Delta State Police Command continue with the chasing.

****

The boys watched the unadorned casket of the man they once knew go down faster than expected. The burial was a brief one, as everyone seemed to disperse as quickly as they had come—briefer condolences to Aunt Roseline, the unfortunate Aunt to be next of kin. She cried the hardest amidst them all, even if it was just pretence. Nobody ever cared for the old man. Even in death, they all shied from their social responsibility of raising his boys. Not that the teenage boys thought they needed any caring for. They didn't like Roseline. Ruke slipped his shoulder off her touch. She'd been crying into his ears by the gravesite. Being next of kin meant she had no choice but play face and take in the boys. The hypocrite! After all this needless showing, she was bound to pass them off to some nitwit before the day was done. That was Roseline. No one needed a psychic to know she never liked the boys. A feeling that went both ways.

The rain stopped falling and she mumbled something to the undertakers—four men with shovels and the dirty business of laying the casket six feet under. It was now officially over so Tagho sauntered off, his eyes hurting from all the hypocrisy. His younger brother quick to follow suit. "Do you think they'll ever catch them?" Ruke asked while they read the epitaphs of great many a fallen man in silence.

Tagho pit two dark expressionless pupils against Ruke, all black and glazed over, visibly irritated by something or someone. someone. someone that wasn't Ruke. "What?—catch who?"

"Dad's killers," Ruke responded, a tear trickling down the younger one's eye.

Tagho feigned a warm smile and stroked off the tear. "You shouldn't cry. The police must have them by now," he lied, fighting off even more liquid accumulating under his own eye. He knocked down Ruke's duffel hat in time, so the lad couldn't see him mopping his own eyes with a piece of the translucent and ceremoniously white satin lace most Urhobos wore at burials. "I'll take you to the station later so you can see for yourself," he'd said with such firmness and rigidity that was almost reassuring.

The younger teen bobbed and helped his elder brother adjust the pink beads adorning his right hand—corals indicating the elder teen was head son of the deceased and crown head of the family the day he turned eighteen. "Do you think she will allow us?" Ruke asked, a little too curiously, "allow us go to the station I mean?"

"Who? Aunt Roseline?"

"Yes her."

Tagho humphed. "Aunt Rosie's gutless—she's definitely not going to keep us, so why wouldn't she?"

The cemetery was empty now. Everyone had vacated the premises save the boys. Roseline had been waiting by a taxi that had patiently endured through the ceremony, but was now overly perturbed about where the boys had vanished to. "Would you two come here before I lose my mind!" she barked the moment she spotted their white and pink visage afar off from across the tombstones.

"She lies you know," Ruke remarked softly.

"I know," Tagho answered and they rubbed knuckles before he tugged Ruke by the shoulder, "come. Let's go to her."

****

The taxi dropped them off for the last time that day at a mechanic's work garage, being the workplace of a very distant relative or an old boyfriend. Whatever the relation, its squeaky gates swung open and the boys chuckled as she led them in.

"What are you boys giggling about?" Aunt Roseline snarled so they went quiet, commuting to eye talk. "You boys wait by the garage while I go meet with your uncle Orido at the office. I'm just upstairs, so don't touch anything," she instructed and disappeared behind a humongous assembly of cars and car parts.

"Orido?" Tagho lifted an eye, "you can see, it's exactly as I said. She's gutless. We'll be alright."

"How are you so sure about that?"

"Why not? Unless you want to wait for a sign from heaven on what's right and wrong?"

"I don't know. I'm thinking we should run?" Ruke suggested.

Tagho humphed. "Run?"

"No, just think about it. Now would be a good time to," Ruke explained as they watched Roseline race up a corridor to discuss with a burly man. A man they'd never met. Or heard of.

"And whom would it be we were running from?" Tagho sniggered, "—her or him?" he asked as a round man took Roseline's hand before peering down at the boys through a small office window.

"I suppose him," Ruke responded and genuflected to greet the man inspecting them through his office window, but the burly man didn't respond. Or even wave at them. He just peered down with a bossy look and Tagho laughed gallantly.

"He's not our dad. We don't have to like him," Tagho mentioned then turned his brother around, and hand in hand they went exploring the work garage. "You don't have a thing to worry about things not working out because if he even messes with us, in the slightest, I'll clunk him," he said putting up a knuckle.

"Just like how you clunked that thug with a monkey wrench?" Ruke rejoined as he met his knuckle with Tagho's.

"Yes, exactly how I clunked that thug with a monkey wrench," he drawled and both brothers shared a laugh.

"No you got your ass whopped that's what happened!" the fourteen year old teased.

"Hmm. Is that so?" came the reply. Being five years and five inches above his brother, Tagho grappled Ruke by the hair and chased him about a decrepit and out-dated motorbike. Laughing and going a few rounds air boxing, both boys played by a gunky mass of steel and a radiator of some sort from one of the broken down Macks in the garage. Ruke clambered atop a smashed generator as king of the world when the boys could hear Roseline arguing from the office above them. It appeared the arrangement upstairs wasn't working out so well for her either.

"You must confess I did dish out some good whopping," Tagho had said when he grew tired of chasing his brother around, which was about the time he spotted it. An easy find because it was the only machine in the work garage not covered in gunk though it had been lying there in the middle of junk and smudge.

"Yes you did!" Ruke roared, "but I still wonder what might have happened if we had caught one of 'em that day. I'm not sure we could both take even the smallest one on with those big muscles he—what is it? What did you find, Tagho?" he asked on discovering he'd been talking with himself all this while because Tagho was already about the hexagonal contraption.

The strange contraption looked like a large capsule—a filthy one, made from a hard plate of some kind. The late teen fingered some dirt off it to expose the polished metal—an element as hard and shiny as titanium. "Come see this," he called, but Ruke was already over before he even called, his curiosity positively burning.

"Looks like it's broken," Ruke said, examining the metallic pile of junk and ready to touch whatever gnawed at his curiosity.

"It's why it's in a mechanic's workshop. Everything's broken here," Tagho retorted, "—and watch the glass, Ruke! You don't want to cut yourself!" he warned for Ruke had motioned to dust off a larger part of the machine with naked hands. Taking Tagho's advice, he simply blew the dust off the contraption instead, and as it turned out the device once had two ground glass lids. One was missing while the other had been shattered through and through. The ground glass still retained fracture lines by its eaves.

"Rostov's per—se—pho—ne," Tagho read out from a murky iron plate tagged to the head of it.

"It has a chamb—there are chambers inside!" Ruke announced," they sorta look like beds. What do you think it is?"

"It's a piece of junk that's for sure," Tagho replied, "looks like a child's plaything."

"You think?"

"I don't think. I know so."

Ruke hummed as he examined the hard paper hoses and rubber tubing behind the contraption. It held wires and three large rotor blades trapped behind some cage or protective shielding. "The iron feels warm back here. Isn't this too..."

"too elaborate?"

"Yes. for a toy, Tagi," Ruke said, genuinely puzzled as he fiddled with one of the torn paper tubing.

"That's what you get with rich people, Ruky. elaborate

toys," Tagho answered before moving on to join his brother behind the shiny machine.

Ruke wiped clear a plate engraved with absurd writings, "it could be alien tech?" he said with a wry grin, almost beaming at his brother with excitement, "that doesn't look like any language we know."

"That. is. the. stupidest. thing. you've said today," Tagho said slowly, deliberately slapping his brother by the nape as Ruke grimaced at him. He pointed out two distinct symbols sandwiched among the other symbols, "that reads 6 ohms, Ruky. Unless your aliens speak Russian or one too many Cyrillic languages?" he scoffed before walking off.

Ruke pouted in disappointment, "I hadn't seen that," he confessed then headed to what he supposed was some sort of door to the contraption. It held no doors. Only an engraving he'd conjectured to conceal a door. "It has no doors," he said to Tagho, only for the elder brother to turn around and find his brother nestled inside Persephone like a cheery canary. The strange contraption held beds in the place of seats.

"What the hell are you doing?" Tagho demanded, scouting the windows upstairs to see if anyone was watching, before looking back down at his brother. Of the mind to give him a good whooping. "Don't let me get to you before you get out of that thing!"

"I'm tired. Do you see any chairs? We have to sit sometime," Ruke said almost stubbornly, easing more into the comfort of the vinyl upholstery and resting his duffel hat across his breasts. The teen's back ached from the day's affairs and his feet felt sore. When Tagho got to the machine, he glowered down at his brother in it. Ruke avoided looking him in the eye, simply casting his gaze elsewhere.

"You get out," Tagho demanded, but weaker in resolve and the early teen could hear it in his voice.

"No," he said tersely. "And I don't think Aunt Roseline's coming down anytime soon," he added wittily, not sure what to expect from those black expressionless pupils fixated on him.

Roseline's voice had steadily increased pitch since the time she and Orido got talking, and unless it lowered, she definitely wasn't done talking. Even the garage, its machines, and the very soil they stood upon was covered in dirt and gunk from motor oil, so it took a minute and three seconds for Tagho to make up his mind and hop into the second chamber. "I see your point," he muttered tastelessly, pitching his back into the vinyl bed. "Feels hard," he said. "What's this? Looks like dried garri?" Tagho mentioned, picking at a caked substance abroad the chamber of what at a time may have been a solution of some sort.

"Eww. it's icky. Could have been baby vomit, you know?" Ruke suggested playfully from his side of the chamber as he fingered off impartial cobwebs from its marine coated interior. "I wonder what it does—or what it was supposed to do. It has like a million buttons," he mentioned, now punching in some dud buttons and not too long after flicking on and off a maze of flip switches across a broad circuit board.

"You're driving me crazy with all that blipping! Keep your fingers to yourself—and don't touch anything!" Tagho warned even as Ruke ruefully grinned at his older brother. The elder brother gave the younger brother the glazed eye, but in taking up the gauntlet, Ruke towered a finger over one more flip switch. Encouraging the puny cockroach would only make him continue, so Tagho turned away. Still, the early teen flicked the switch and Tagho seemed to ignore this minor act of will. However when Ruke had settled into his seat, allowing things to stay quiet for a while, Tagho pounced on the defiant little roach.

Snorting and air boxing, the brothers hardly took note of the level red button they depressed though they took notice of a ruptured air pipe—more like a internal vacuum pipe that belched a wind of dust into both their faces. The applied mascara skewered their semblance to something off the Eyo Masquerades at the Eko Festival, and Tagho sneezed heavily even as Ruke chortled, "appears some part of it still works!"

Tagho cleaned his face and whatever could be cleaned off his white attire, "this is going to be hard to wash off," he muttered as both brothers retired into the vinyl bed for a more comforting number of minutes, "consider yourself lucky, you."

They lay there; Ruke taking time to wipe the dust off his face and his attire when Tagho suggested a little while later, "we can lie in silence, Rukewe. What's with the humming?"

Ruke raised a brow. "What humming?"

"Don't lie to me —you forget I'm older than you," Tagho retorted but Ruke shrugged.

"I'm not humming."

"then i guess it's me 'cause who else?" Tagho rejoined in trenchant sarcasm.

"Beats me," Ruke answered offhandedly, "I not aware of anything you're saying i've done."

He realized his brother was telling the truth. It was not like Ruke to drag a lie into an argument. "There's this strange droning coming from where I lay my head," Tagho confessed and that was when they noticed it. "Come to think of it, now I feel—is that a red light?" he asked quickly.

"What red light?" Ruke asked back and turned to the panel of buttons to discern a sublime red light flickering behind a sheet of dust that had accumulated across some kind of screen. He wiped down the dusty screen with his bare hands just in time for the brothers to discover a set of unchanging numbers beneath a timer actively counting down, reading 00:05, 00:04, 00:03, 00:02 and impulsively Tagho jolted to sitting up, glowering at his brother from his end of the chamber.

"You've turned it on," he said and Ruke smiled sheepishly at 00:01.

"At least the toy still works," he answered wittily as the timer hit 00:00, but sandwiched between seconds Ruke had prime sitting to witness firsthand what Persephone had been invented to do. The machine eviscerated Tagho in a puff of smoke; the elder brother's very figure baked dry by lightning to nothing but ash clouds within the second it took a person to blink. Ruke stood aghast as the blood in his veins dried up and his body went numb, confused and frozen in thought. Everything about him, his organs, his bones, his entire essence, desiccated to the scorch of the lightning in his chamber—and like his brother, disintegrating into nothing. All Persephone left of both boys were ash clouds. Not a wick of their hair survived the titanium machine.

green earth

Her face was all blurred and wonky like peering down the ground glass the way she did. The little blonde clad in white wiped down on the mist that'd saturated the lid and gave the hard glass a tenuous rap. The sound reverberated through the chamber, racking both ears at full volume. So loudly, the early teen found himself banging against the glass lid and gasping for air. "Am I dead?!—I'm dead!— I'm coffined!" he panicked as the lid refused to budge. He could see a girl on the other side of the glass trying to communicate, but the chamber was just too small to contain his thoughts—he was trapped, in the contraption or whatever it was. He couldn't hear a word. The little blonde pressed herself against the chamber and gave it a slight jab from the outside—and that was all it took for the glass to levitate itself automatically on one hinge. Ruke leaped out of the crazy contraption and onto the desert floor on all fours, gasping for air like a pup. More air.

"You don't listen. You're not going to survive long if you don't listen, knucklehead," the girl said, arms akimbo, and pouting her lips.

The scorching sand slowly cooked his hands and knees. "Ahh! Ahh! Arhh!" Ruke screamed, yet he was too weak to move a muscle so he let both hands broil in the sand.

"Pytrice, what' you found?" a voice called from the distance.

"two knuckleheads about the machines, ol'pops—" the

twelve-year old answered before noticing the strange apparel about the dark-skinned boy, "boys from someplace—I don't know—wherever," she demurred and proceeded to unhook the second chamber. Its handle was oxidized and impossible to pry open from the outside, so she took a moment to signal the other someone inhabiting inside. The second chamber unhinged itself, and its ground glass lifted robotically. "This one listens," she mentioned, and now really getting to notice the see-through attire and strangely pink beads this one wore as he ventured out of the chamber. "what are you supposed to be dressed as?" she asked because today was hot. Sincerely hot. But he seemed wobbly on his feet, so she handed him her gun and propped him up until he found his centre. Tagho took the titanium gun without a second thought to what it was, even as Ruke sprung at him carelessly with borrowed strength. The shorter one took a moment to cry which made the little blonde snicker.

A bleach-haired old man in a shiny lab coat came at them on what appeared to be a scooter. He was with a mechanical eye of some sort, "I can't believe I'm seeing this—humans of blackened skin? And here, I had thought your race was extinct," he stated excitedly, almost unable to contain himself as he approached with the scooter, leaping with one foot. He laughed loudly and into the air when getting off his scooter, as he offered both boys, both men that is, an overgenerous handshake. "Haku and Hrth!" he named them as he shook them, but not consciously letting saliva drool down his lips the way it did. He looked crazy as he took their hands ecstatically. "The prophecies are true!" he shouted beyond their faces, laughing, and then turned towards the brown sky to shout it out again. It was really a golden brown sky up there, and both Tagho and Ruke had blank expressions. When he was done, the old man came around to introducing himself.

"I'm a scientist. You can call me Meeko—Scientist Meeko—Doctor Meeko—Meeko the Physicist— whatever you like," he said, catching up on the drool and wiping his face completely off it. But, not the smile. The smile remained smack across his warty face. And ever generously.

"He looks dangerous," Ruke leaned away from the crazy scientist and towards his brother.

"I know. Doesn't look like all his buttons are together," Tagho mentioned calmly. He hadn't just said that because of the old man's unbuttoned lab coat. He was unsure why an old man with a strange titanium apparatus made of two glass lenses affixed to his right eye would be gloating at them. Nor had the much late teen any clue to what was going on. Or how they got here. This place didn't look like home. In fact, it didn't feel right despite it was midday with the right amount of sunlight shining through. The clouds over them were a baked brown with dancing auroras above them! Auroras!

There was a weird silence after his very brief introduction. The brothers stared blankly at him as he stared blankly at them, still wearing that broad smile. A smile the boys were forced to emulate.

"Forgive me, I know it's awkward to stare at you—but if you know what—my god, is that cotton you're wearing?—no, can't be! That's a good replica," he demurred then turned to Pytrice euphorically, "the prophecies are true, petridish—to have counted it all as crazy?" the scientist giggled, "I should be ashamed of myself! Ashamed!"

The little blonde sought to size up the visitors. "Humph." She didn't look impressed.

"Where—where exactly are we?" Tagho asked.

The scientist was quick to the reply, "oh, yes. Forgive me. You came in that," he pointed to the machine, "not to worry. You're at 2021AD, and that's a space-time displacement machine," he said brilliantly and both boys raised their eyes to such a queer answer. "—it's a teleportation device," he'd explained on meeting their distant expressions.

The little blonde stamped her feet impatiently grabbing at her blond hair in frustration, "it's a time machine, knuckleheads! that's what ol'pops is trying to say!" she butt in and both boys gave the twelve year old the glazed eye. She didn't look intimidated.

"eh—in a way—or so to speak. That's a very crude definition though. But yes, it somewhat operates like a time machine," Meeko grinned even as Tagho scratched his head with the titanium toy. He hadn't the slightest idea of how to approach their present predicament. And from what he and his brother had witnessed constantly across the streets of Warri, mental illness was a volatile thing to tackle.

"What year are you from?" Meeko asked eagerly, before interrupting himself to request politely, "would you mind?—would you mind if I take that thing from you?"

Tagho handed over the titanium tool, and Meeko frowned at Pytrice, "this is for protection," he mumbled at her.

"What?—a storm's approaching. Crawlers hardly come out in a storm," she fought back. "FYI, let's not forget your silver rule."

The old man seemed to look across the strange desert horizon with askance. The boys looked on with him. If this old lunatic was in anyway right and they were not hapless prisoners in some strange desert, there seemed to be sand particles in the wind and a black geodesic dome a long distance to their far right. "It's not safe we remaining here in the open," Meeko said hurriedly and jumped on his scooter, or hovering gismo, for as Ruke had come to notice the device had never for once made contact with the ground. That simple fact would have been very easy to overlook if the early teen wasn't awed by it.

"To where? We don't know where we are. Or how we got here. Where are you taking us?" Tagho challenged the old man bravely, unwilling to be dragged blindly into some untold captivity. These two were obviously white.

Meeko seemed to shut off the device and it fell to the

ground. Tagho noticed that. "If you tell me what year you're from, maybe I can answer that—"

"2007," Ruke answered, "We are Nigerians."

The old man stood a bit puzzled, "Nigerians? What's that?" he asked, and very sincerely too. Both boys gaped, seeming to lose control of their jaws and wit within the second.

"Nigeria is a country," Ruke argued, not knowing how that helped.

"Oh," he sighed sheepishly, "we don't have those anymore."

"What?"

"Yea, we don't," he said and not too apologetic about it, "you say you're 2007, which era was it?—I mean, is it? Is it AA, AD, AI? What era did you travel through to get here?"

"AD," Ruke replied, a bit unsure about his answer.

"twenty-07 ad desolates? That's not likely. Your kind has been long extinct before even 10-07 Ad Desolatus," the old man demurred, frequently on the lookout for something. Be it the horizon. Worrying the more they tarried in this desert. "We shouldn't be talking out here—"

"I want to go inside, ol'pops," the little blond Pytrice interrupted brusquely, swinging her titanium toy in the air on being bored to death, "your silver rule is we shouldn't be out long. You're breaking your silver rule, you realize that ol'pops?!"

"Yes I realize that," he responded tersely, even as Tagho sought to correct the scientist.

"ad desolatus?—what's that? No, it's Anno Domini."

When Tagho had said that, even Pytrice felt the impact of his words like the explosion of a million barrels of TNT. Meeko could have said something, but he didn't. No one knew it as that anymore. Though he might have mentioned it once or twice in his lifetime. Not even Pytrice. Or so Meeko thought.

"Isn't that the era of the flare, ol'pops? You're liars. You're making things up—no way—" she jeered, though she noticed the helm of both their attires had a translucent fabric that felt gritty to touch. "This isn't cotton," she grunted and tossed the fabric away, "liars."

"Believe us," Ruke said to her and Tagho could draw up no explanation why he offered her his hat. Pytrice took the hat from him beaming with anxiety as she felt its nap and its woolly interior, "Dad mentioned—what does this mean, ol' pops? It can't be, can't it?" she asked Meeko.

Meeko's mechanical eyes seemed to lock in on the pink beads the elderly one wore. It was proof of water, so he didn't speak. A tear rolled down his eyes, "—this isn't supposed to be mathematically possible."

"What isn't possible?" Hrth demanded, but had other concerns on his mind.

"We have to get you two out of here to somewhere safe. Your time is beyond anybody," he stated.

Pytrice passionately pushed the boys to motion as Meeko activated his scooter. The device levitated him above the sands.

"What do you mean our time is beyond anybody?" Ruke asked, a bit more seriously now.

"There's a lot i have to tell you, but know that you're in Loess—we call her sand land," Meeko answered, "it's still earth, your earth, but millions of generations past your time. That date you mentioned, the day you're from, we only know those from index references inside historic archives, so if what you're telling me is true, you're the only ones alive who've seen green earth."

"What is green earth?" he asked but Tagho butt in.

"If this is earth, why does it feel different?" he asked, a bit unsure why he asked in the first place but Meeko was more than elated to answer.

"It's true then. The two of you really are from there, 'cause only limited archives tell gravity was different in your time—the oldest archives," he said, a lot of excitement and yet anxiety in his eyes, "do not worry about the wooziness. You'll get used to it in time. As for the tinkering light-footedness you're feeling now, we'll adjust to gravity one at the facility," he counselled and beamed broadly at them; making an attempt to placate the boys.

"I don't feel any differently," Ruke replied as they walked across the sands and Meeko stopped the hovering gismo.

"Show them Pytrice," was all he had to say for the little blonde to stamp her foot and displace the sand by her feet. The golden sands lifted as a swirl; in nothing less than a spellbinding array of particles suspended weightlessly in the air!

"Welcome to Sand Land. It takes about two to three minutes for sand to settle here so you'd better watch those eyes," she announced without interest.

surrogate reality

Meeko did away with the scooter when they reached the hatch; a copper lid, flat to the ground and indistinguishably buried within the golden sands, leading down a ladder ten feet into solid earth and built to be impregnable. It was very well impossible to spot from the outside, unless you already knew where it was. As Meeko did.

The little blonde keyed in a string of codes for the lid to yank itself open. She kicked away the sands and held it open, but when Ruke set himself upon it, she shouldered him off. And bristly too. In fact, she scowled at him and he remained knocked for six until Meeko set himself upon the hatch. He watched her let the old man take his time climbing down, taking custody of his scooter and giving him all the support he needed. It was only after Meeko was safely down the ladder, did she allow Tagho go down the hatch, then biting her lips after Tagho was done with the ladder as if contemplating the odds of keeping Ruke out. After a brief eternity of staring at each other however, she snarled, "don't waste my time. We don't have all day." And Ruke found himself agreeing with the girl with the gun. Aside the fact, he'd been staring at her teeth the whole time. So she put one to his shoulder on his way down.

"ouwwl it's okay. I'm sorry," he apologized because she had poor dentition, and apparently was sensitive about that.

"Welcome to the INS Center. This place is a nuclear shielded research centre from the old days, but it's part of what we call The Facility. We have all we need here from sleeping quarters, medical quarters to laboratories—" Meeko announced proudly when both boys had gotten off the ladder into the mega-steel facility, "—reactor rooms, an observation room for astronomical research and more. It's huge, isn't it? This is a small part of the whole thing."

The boys hadn't realized they'd all been sweating until now. The conditioned air was disparately cool, free of particles, and had a faint charge that soothe the nostrils.

"Whoa! Are we underground?" Ruke asked, mesmerized by the neon lights illuminating every corner of the massive facility, and the fluorescent lights straddling every curb.

"No," Pytrice answered in mordacious rejoinder, acting tough by hopping off the ladder from a precarious height. She sauntered to shelve the titanium gun in what appeared to be a small munitions shelf protected behind a tough wall of aventurine glass. She also powered down the scooter and shelved it when a cat came to her; the hairy white cat had been lurching behind the corners for a while.

"Yes Haku. This entire facility is built underground, save the observatory—" Meeko answered politely before directing his attention at one of many display screens jutting from formidable steel walls. After punching into one of the display screens a set of executable codes, a different colour of light flickered on; green LED lights flashing concurrently and something seemed to lock in place beneath their feet, the earth feeling strangely firm and stronger.

"Pytrice try and keep Kyno away from the boys," Meeko said fondly.

"My feet feel heavy," Ruke mentioned and old Meeko smiled.

"It's standard 95rev per minute, Haku—gravity one that's the gravity of your time, isn't it? I thought you'd feel more at home if I set it to one," Meeko replied and the brothers acted to understand even a piece of any of this.

"Why do you call us Haku and Hrth when we haven't given you our names?" Ruke asked sincerely, no longer of the opinion the old man with the lens across the eye was all crazy.

"Everyone knows who are. You're Haku," he said with wonderment before turning to Tagho, "—and you are Hrth. You are both sons of the prophecy, the birthing of our surrogate reality."

"No. No. No. You don't understand. This is all happenstance. We just happened by here," the older brother cut in briskly, "—and in that damned thing," he said when he spotted the very same contraption that had transported them there nestled in a glass compartment at the heart of the facility like a display exhibit.

Meeko looked at the machine and smiled broadly at the brothers, "that's the INS Lab and I have already explained to you what that is. Whatever way you got here, it's no mistake you are here with us now. And with me at this time! It is as the prophecy foretells," Meeko stated plainly.

"This one hardly looks like one who can save the world," Pytrice said as she moseyed about the fourteen year old with her cat in hand. She punched him again and Haku flinched, "and if the prophecy is true, shouldn't this one have wings?" she taunted as Tagho glowered at her. She wasn't going to punch him now. She wouldn't dare.

Meeko harrumphed. "that's simply a metaphor, petridish," he answered, pulling Pytrice and her cat away from upsetting the boys, "actually I'm a scientist, I not supposed to believe in prophecies but not until I saw you two today," he stated.

"I'm sorry to pop your balloon, Mr or is it Dr Meeko. I'm trying to absorb this all very quickly, but not much of what's going is making much sense to me. I am no protector. We are not here to save anyone's world. I just want to know how I can get him safely home or back to wherever you think we came from—if you can help us, that is?" Tagho requested politely but Meeko seemed ever the more excited to hear him talk like that.

"Back home?—what home? Is aunt Roseline our home?" Haku challenged Hrth out of the blue and his eyes grew moist. "Dad's dead, we have no home," he had said even as Hrth tried to mop those eyes dry, but

Haku wouldn't let him, shoving the older one's arm aside, "don't touch me. I can take care of myself," he barked and the older one frowned. They were brothers and Meeko gloated over the discovery of it.

"Boys and fights," Pytrice humphed, but something seemed to shift in Hrth and his countenance changed.

"If you say we are in the future, does that mean that if you were to send us back you can send us to a time before we left?" he asked after a moment and suddenly both brothers seemed to lock eyes in coded communication.

"No, not the future. The future is only a coming together of our actions like your being here—but the answer is yes, you could put it that way. You making it here from your time was the harder part. Sending you back wouldn't be difficult," Meeko said and Haku beamed as Horus on its very first day.

"So what is this prophecy?" Hrth asked.

"I had wanted to show you boys to your rooms so you'd have a bit of nourishment and some time to yourselves before sharing this with you but I see no need for that now," Meeko replied and for the first time today the old man took off the titanium mechanism attached to his eye and bleached hair. It cut his years back by a decade and made him less likely to come from a loony bin. Meeko led the boys towards the centre of the facility, "If you are 2007 your time, then on the twenty first of the fifth, 2015, still your time, it is recorded your sun spiked prematurely and underwent a cataclysmic split rather than go supernova—with no ample warning of course to the indigenous population. The damage the colossal explosion inflicted was nigh absolute to all forms of life on the planets. An infinitely better fate, had it gone supernova. The halves from the split we now call Ra and Horus, but the earth in particular was subject to an anomaly of EM and particle radiation for more than half a day from both suns."

They ambled past a small circular craft on their way to the centre of the facility. It was floating above what appeared to be a miniaturized helipad, and the helipad itself bordered a massive channel—some sort of inlet that appeared to continue endlessly. The inlet even broke out in branches in the far distance.

"What's that?" Haku asked as he ogled the small craft.

"That's a hoverbot," Pytrice answered glumly.

"A hoverbot," he chimed, "what does it do?"

"It hovers," she derided and ambled past him. This one was just too slow in the head for her company.

"That hoverbot's been with us for generations, Haku. One of Pytrice's great great grandfathers invented it. We use the hoverbot to travel the channels," Meeko answered kindly as they walked right across the mouth of the gargantuan tunnel leading someplace out of sight, "the INS Center is one big unit but we tend to numerate. That entrance, the part you just came from, we call unit 5. But this is unit 8. It's the terminal gateway, and this, this huge cavern you see is just one of four channels that access the Alpha wings. If you follow the axis that leads right, that will lead you to the greenhouse. The greenhouse is where we synthesize food and drugs for the facility—" he lectured and Meeko put his hand against a biometric scanner that served as a door handle for two huge blast doors to close off the inlet. He frowned at Pytrice for reasons best known to them, "one leads to the reactor, another to the infirmary, and finally the observatory. We are on our way there—" he pointed just ahead, "there we call centre control. Or simply unit 15."

"Are there other facilities like this one?" Hrth asked and Meeko nodded.

At the centre, amid humongous panes of protective glass that divided the INS in parts, lay the largest of the screens, not standing upright but welded flat against a table and having green light feeding it from beneath. Meeko tapped on the icons embossed into the rim of the screen and the entire table tinkered and shot up in a 3D hologram of the galaxy. A high 3D resolution of the Milky Way.

"This is the galaxy you knew. It's the galaxy before the day we call Ragnarök—the end of life—Judgment Day," Meeko said flatly and Haku and Hrth had a distant look on their faces. He zoomed into a view of the earth and the planetary system. The moment he hit an icon, an automated illustration played in loop. "As you can see, both suns microwaved a good part of the earth, almost sterilizing it of life. The survivors from the blast of particle radiation had to endure periodic solar flares from Horus. Horus to this day is the more reactive of the two suns and once in a while discharges a blast of charged particles. Ra, on the other hand, is more stable. Does make one suspicious that solar anomalies ended life on Mars and the other planets, millions of years ago," Meeko digressed, hoping they understood nearly half of the information he was shooting right at them. Both boys seemed to nod glumly.

"What you're saying is everyone dies?" Haku asked, only for Hrth to tap his younger brother by the nape a second time today. or after millions of years.

"—I'd meant back home," Ruke snapped at his brother, angry and offended he would do that here. In face of total strangers.

The little blonde chortled. "best wish that one good luck," she snickered, so Meeko required she set up rooms to accommodate them, in a bid to keep her from further upsetting the boys, "that one, that one doesn't listen at all, ol'pops," she further announced even as she left to go animate their rooms.

"Sorry about Pytrice. That's just how she is," the doctor apologized ruefully after she left. So to skip the oddity, he continued his explanation, "No. Not everyone dies, Haku. Or everything. A considerable number of people survived in the continents. Your continent in particular. And fortunately for our kind, a better of that number were intelligent people surviving at government and private installations similar to ours, but that was before the crawlers when we still had an earth to govern. Our numbers have steadily declined since then. And I don't just mean the grounds alone. The greatest damage however were to the oceans—water being the essence of the life on this planet. I heard this planet was once 74% water by composition?" he stated or asked, and with fascination, but the brothers didn't know how to respond to that.

"Yes, it was, or is," Hrth responded heavily, "we call it the ocean."

"Incredible."

"Why? What's the figure now?"

"6%, but that's all literature," Meeko said glumly.

"Why do you say that?"

"because that water, our 6%, is either irradiated or locked in pockets someplace. We barely have enough to synthesize our drinking water nowadays," he stated flatly and their jaws dropped a second time, "you're both lucky to have actually seen it, you know. It must have been a beautiful thing, the ocean."

"So basically what you're telling us is, even if we go back now we'd be dead in say seven-eight years," Hrth inferred grimly.

"Eh...yes, in a way, but no—not according to the prophecy you would."

"I don't get it," Ruke said.

"Neither do I," Hrth concurred.

So, Meeko followed suit with what could be said was his half of the story. "I don't know how it started, but for

41

generations a secret message has been communicated by hearsay. We know it as the message of a surrogate reality. As it happens, it's a prophecy that has evolved through hundreds and hundreds of versions, still all the stories basically tell of two travellers of alien origin—a noble one, Haku, riding on the wings of a winged protector, his warrior bird, Hrth, and soaring over the seas to stop our extinction. According to the prophecy, since only the alien actually set foot on green earth, only the alien can set foot on it again to restore to us what was once lost by propelling us and sending us soaring into the skies," he said and the brothers could read the excitement in the eyes. "Some versions say we literally take the sky, but that's all subject to interpretation. The prophecy goes on to say that if our feet remain on the ground, our fate will be sealed and we will ultimately perish as a species, facing an inevitable end."

"We're not aliens," Hrth replied, and Meeko smiled.

"I know. Let's just say we figured that part of the prophecy out ourselves when we invented that," Meeko said, pointing to the time-displacement machine, "but you're travellers. You can't deny that and your race has been long extinct, but here you are. Two sons of the ebony race before me. I told you. The prophecy is all subject to interpretation."

"And what if you're wrong?"

Meeko was quiet for a while, allowing himself some time to muse, "actually, many scientists frowned at the whimsical nature of the prophecy when it was first heard—called it a flight of fantasy, a false hope. Only a handful of scientists chose to believe in fate. I think they liked the versions that tell of our kind conquering the galaxy. But none of our early fathers thought that was remotely even possible, they called it wishful thinking because things were better then. That was before the crawlers appeared in the Reanimation Era and we became desperate. The prophecy grew to legend over the last thousand years and became our one only hope because even if it was a forlorn hope, hope itself has a way of changing everything you never believed achievable. Now the crawlers are taking over. We've been trying to survive ever since. Even Rostov, and his grandfather, believed the stories till their demise—" he said and kind of drifted away in thought behind a forlorn face.

"Dr. Meeko?" Haku called soberly and the old man returned to them, "did you know Ros—tov?"

"Certainly. Every scientist knows Rostov. He was a brilliant physicist. In fact, it was one of Rostov's great great great grandfathers who drew the schematics for the first time-displacement machine. We owe many things we know now to that great line of great men," he said warmly, "still, my acquaintance with him was one of a more personal arrangement because he was also Pytrice's godfather before the accident at Tech lab, or the unfortunate crawler incident that overran his facility in the east islands," he said sadly, "—how that feels like a lifetime ago."

"Then he owned Persephone," Haku stated softly.

"Yes, his great grandfathers did and passed it down the—how did you come about that name?" Meeko interrupted himself, looking knocked for six as he stared at the brothers. Still, he hadn't waited for an answer before laughing. And laugh he did. "That stubborn old bum did it. He finally did it!"

Haku and Hrth let the old man pull them in his arms basking in the euphoria of whatever delighted him. "I'm sure the ol' buffoon mocks me from beyond the grave," the physicist chided himself, "if you have Persephone, we have not a moment to lose!" he said and worked up a strange algorithm on all the screens.

It'd taken a while in coming, but there'd been a question lingering at the back of Tagho's mind for a while now. So Hrth asked directly, there wasn't need for any embellishments, "what are crawlers?" he demanded and the old man harrumphed.

"I'll handle the crawlers, you just stay out of my way," Pytrice interrupted from behind. She'd been standing right behind Hrth with her cat, two remote keys, and separate fluffy sponges in hand. She depressed a blue button on the remotes and a pair of cylinders in the walls opened up. "Those are your rooms, and these are yours," she handed Hrth a key and sponge before tossing the other key and sponge to Haku. "Depress the purple button to deactivate the rooms," she instructed.

"How are we to clean up?—Meeko said you don't have any water here?" Ruke asked.

"You don't need water to use that," the little blonde smirked.

crawlers

In the time it took Hrth to change into synthetic clothes and return, the twelve year old blonde had pieced together a very large gun. The display screens at the facility blinked red, highlighting a minuscule section of an arcane schematic.

"What's going on?" Hrth asked, distrustful to the little girl with the big gun.

"It's none of your biz!" she shot back, biting her lips and picking Kyno up in her arms.

"We need to disable the machines outside. Seeing that we've had no hiccups since you arrived, we need to make certain we preserve the novel timeline—a precaution to prevent any incidents," Meeko stated, handing Pytrice a pair of goggles. "Rostov activated that old time-displacement machine because it was the one he was familiar with. We haven't used the outside wing for experiments in years, so the equipment is off and inevitably not of much good."

"Is she going up there alone?" Hrth inferred, but his concern struck a chord with the blonde.

"I said it's none of your biz," she smouldered and activated the gun.

"Good point. I was so carried away I forgot the golden rule," Meeko concurred and Pytrice flushed red. "Find Hrth some gravity boots. He should go with you..."

"I'll be fine on my own," she protested but Meeko would

hear none of it.

"Fine." She pouted.

"And what's this golden rule?" Tagho asked Meeko even as the little blonde shouldered her way past him. "Stay out of my way," she stated resentfully.

"It's that we go out in pairs. Don't take what she says to heart," Meeko answered civilly, seeking to redress her lack of tact.

"appears she isn't afraid of anything," Hrth remarked, watching the twelve year old trample her way away, not the least bit offended by her.

Meeko chortled. "That's just how she is. Can be a tough cookie," he stated and sought to attend to the blinking screen.

"So how's all this possible? I was always of the opinion time travel was out of bounds technology?" Hrth asked, leaning into the large table. "In our time, it was essentially fiction we see at theatres."

"Theatres—" Meeko parroted with fascination, "that's art, is it not? 'read about those. 'must have been lovely," he said. "Like I said earlier, we don't call it time travel, Hrth, because it's not an echo of the past. More like time jump or displacement. It's not a truly complicated principle when you look at it. We've known this for a long time, it just we've not been properly motivated to put all together until we had to. Even in your time, Einstein postulated that space and time were distinct continuums when he discovered the equivalence of mass and energy and put up the relativity theory—the E equals mc2 equation where m is mass and c is—"

"the speed of light," Hrth answered and chuckled after seeing Meeko's polished face, "give me some credit, ol'pops—they teach that in schools."

"I can see that," Meeko said with a smile, "and it appears you've taken a liking to Pytrice—that's her language. Then you should also know Einstein postulated that anything that travels faster than light travels through time. Care to know why?" Meeko had asked, but hadn't waited for a reply, "because matter or mass occupies space. In actual fact, it basically is a property of space itself! So for years, it baffled us what energy does occupy."

"Time?" Hrth inferred.

"Right," the old man cheered. "You see somewhere along the line, Rostov's grandparents proposed that matter could never travel faster than light. The lucid reason being that light is simply energy and has negligible to no mass, but matter does—so if matter was ever to occupy time, it could only do so after becoming energy."

"Which brings the relevance of the equation," Hrth added.

"Right," Meeko affirmed. "It's what Rostov's great grandfather created Persephone to do—the transpositional conversion of matter into energy, which is easier said than done because you had to direct that energy by the light-year once you're done creating it. A light-year being the—"

"distance it takes light to travel one year," Hrth help finish the fact.

"—in a vacuum, but right," the old man affirmed again. "Within that distance, we discovered light skips time. Ultimately a gap of about ten years, which we chose to call the 10-year Aggregate that now becomes like a portal to us—a time bridge when you convert that energy back to matter. In essence, what I'm trying to explain to you is that energy folds space. Not real space—we found out that's just impossible, but space on a wholly different continuum—a time continuum."

"This should be your size," Pytrice uttered and dropped a pair of heavy boots in a thud. It was time for business.

"I'd allow Hrth handle the plasma neurolizer, don't you think?" Meeko suggested as he set in place his eye apparatus.

But Pytrice snapped at him, "no! Why would you even suggest that, ol'pops!" then grimaced at Hrth, "he doesn't even know how to use it. Here, you can watch Kyno while we're up there," she shoved Hrth her white cat and led the way to the hatch. Kyno was the atypical Balinese feline evolved to trap sands in her fur but Hrth handed over the white cat to the scientist, trading it in for a pair of goggles.

"Just keep her safe," Meeko mouthed, but all Hrth could do was smile wryly.

This little blonde was sure to be a handful.

****

The steel cylinders slid open and Haku emerged in synthetic flax. With his brother nowhere in sight, it kind of made a little sense to ask, "where is he?"

"up one level with Pytrice," Meeko answered, inferring above ground but seldom taking his eyes off whatever mathematical stunt he was pulling across the screens, "Hrth's helping restore the complex—we don't want anything mucking up your timeline."

"our timeline?" Haku asked as he requested a place to sit.

Meeko rapped on the hologram table, indicating it was built sturdy enough to prop his paltry weight. Haku set himself upon its edge and waited for Meeko to tear himself off the screen, although the scientist didn't have to take the eye apparatus off this time because the mechanized lenses simply parted, giving way to the scientist's true eye. "A bridge—your personal time bridge," he answered, distancing his arms in reference and watching Haku's face light up like a lithium flashlight. "You jumped from one machine to our machine—that's a bridge. From your date to our date— that's a time bridge or timeline," he explained. "Whoever has knowledge of your source-time coordinates can take advantage of that information—even alter the bridge itself! if that ever happens this whole thing is undone and we're screwed, which is the one and vital reason you boys have to take that piece of information with you to the grave," he stated flatly, turning to sequence more data into the supercomputer, "—that reminds me, I'll be needing those source-time coordinates if I have to trace Persephone and beam you back as I should."

"But you just said..."

"we'll make this a onetime exception," the old scientist replied sheepishly, "the coordinates, please?"

He got a distant look from Haku.

"—what I mean is you need to give me the precise location and date you left your era," Meeko said, having to explain further.

"the date's August, the seventh," Haku replied boldly, but shrugged afterwards, "—I think? I'm sorry, 'twas kind of a date I got at a glance from yesterdays headline," he apologized. "We came after that day, but I can swear the month's August."

Meeko took the swift conjecture with a pinch of salt. "Err...August is the eight month. I think we can work with that. It'll probably take me a week or two to pinpoint your precise date of departure, so it's not too much work," he answered and keyed a variable into the computer, "and the location?" Meeko inquired softly.

"Warri, Nigeria. It's in Africa our era," the child blurted very confidently.

"No—yes, but no. I mean I'm asking for the true location. I'm asking you for the true location now. You know, your longitude, latitude? Altitude? Or whatever indexes it is you used?" the scientist asked again, hoping he was getting across.

"O...k...the longitude and latitude for Warri is what you're asking?" Haku asked back, hitting the doldrums with a bang and licking his lips. "I don't think I know the longitude and latitude, Dr. Meeko. And I don't think my brother does either," he said ruefully.

"O...k...that shouldn't be a problem finding," Meeko lied and holographed a strange map, its geodic outline seldom bearing any semblance to planet Earth until the scientist adjusted an index and altered the continental patterns just enough for Africa to come in sight. "This is a map of Loess, I had to realign polarity—aside adjusting for continental drift and magnetic core displacement, to set the earth the way it was in your era," he explained, but he seemed to have lost the child somewhere inside the explanation, so the scientist went right on to ask, "can you now show me where this Warri-Nigeria is? Go ahead. You can touch it."

Haku roughly fingered the location between the gulf of guinea and lake Chad so the 3D hologram automatically shaded down and keyed in the index information of 6° 22'N : 2° 46'E , 13° 22'N : 13° 40'E before an invisible computer read out Estimated Target Area: 356,669 squares miles, Highest point: Chappal Waddi, 2.419 km as it shot out the evaluation data across the screens. Meeko whistled, "Impossible. That's too much land mass to scan, even for this computer. Neither do we have the time, or resources if I could figure out a way," he hesitated to say, "isn't there anyway you can narrow the search parameters down to where this Warri-Nigeria is?"

"No, that's Nigeria, Dr. Meeko," Ruke informed, "but this

is Warri," the early teen fingered a location to the south of the borderline, and the computer automatically keyed in the new box parameters 5° 31′N : 5° 44′E, 5° 29′ N, 5° 46′ E. It was the best he could do under such pressing circumstances.

"That's better," Meeko heaved in relief, "—still a lot of land mass though. What's the altitude?"

"Altitude, Dr Meeko?"

"You don't have it?"

"No."

"These are all sets of numbers you could easily have noticed inside the machine, Haku?"

"We didn't know."

Meeko sighed. "My guessimate is three months before we can find, calibrate, and synchronize the machines for your return," he said and it was Ruke's turn to whistle.

"3 months? I don't think my brother will be willing to stay here that long, Dr. Meeko. Is there any way you could get us back before then?"

"Unless you want to tell me Hrth knows the exact time-source coordinates to Persephone's location?" Meeko asked pointedly.

"No—I guess not. We never really bothered about paying attention to such stuff," he replied.

"Then he'll have to wait," Meeko said matter-of-factly, "besides, it's a good thing. We can make use of the 3 months because you'll need time to synergize, Haku.

You're the special one. There's a wealth of information you have to take back with you, and people you haven't met yet."

"You just said people, Dr. Meeko. You mean you have people in this facility?—as in live people?" Haku couldn't help but ask. He had to be certain he'd heard correctly for they'd spent hours in the facility and it looked deserted. In actual fact, this facility was deserted.

Meeko set up a comm. link and pushed record to real-time mail, "of course, we have people here. Whatever gave you the wrong impression?"

****

The plasma neurolizer had a fuel source like something off the Frigid Zone. It was intensely cold and Hrth could feel the gun chill the air.

"So what are we supposed to do when we get up there?" he asked, trying not to act concerned over a twelve year old with a big gun. Or the light way she went about the ladder with the gun in hand. Or that its ominous blue light glowered into his face from above.

She didn't think he was worth the data, but Pytrice fed it to him anyway. "You'll see," she mentioned when she keyed in the codes and the golden sands came pouring in. The hatch lifted itself vertically and they exited to meet a raging storm—an intense sand storm with twisters. The sands tore immediately at the goggles and the synthetic flax they wore. Hrth stared at the brown clouds suspended high up in the sky above them— wondering what their dark nature held or what the ominous lightning trailing the storm portended. He had a tingling sensation in his feet as they proceeded to the machines. Something just didn't feel right about doing this now.

"It's a magnetic storm," she answered glumly before he'd asked, "and yes it's dangerous—we try to avoid coming out here in a storm, but priorities are priorities."

"No water, but I see clouds," Hrth mumbled after her.

"You do see the twisters, don't you? That's sand up there, not water," she retorted and Hrth took offense.

"You talk tough for a girl. Still you're too young to be handling a gun, you do know that, don't you?" Hrth shot at her and she scowled at him.

"And you're too old to be scared of a simple storm," she shot back.

Even with the winds against them, they made it to the machines. Both time-displacement machines looked operational so Pytrice proceeded to dislodge their fuel cells from behind, the handy twelve year old being quite the mechanic. She uncased their protective shielding and bagged both fuel cells, yet never for once letting go of the gun. Hrth had noticed. She let him pick up the bag when she was done; for aside the sands getting into everything, the fuel cells made quite the weight when together.

"So what's your gun supposed to do?" Hrth popped the ever pressing question, a question lingering at the back of his mind ever since she'd pieced the large gun together, so she directed the plasma neurolizer at him.

"ha-ha very funny."

She shouldered the neurolizer and answered succinctly, "it shoots a stream of white light."

"like a laser gun?"

"No, just light," she snapped, already exasperated with the dialogue.

"Just light? that's it? No lasers? No bullets?"

The little blonde rolled her eyes at him.

"Oh, it's intended to blind not kill your enemy. Quite thoughtful," Hrth jeered, but the twelve year old knew a thing or two about sarcasm.

"Lasers cause too much collateral damage and capped projectiles don't work on crawlers—" she parroted defensively, and by the sound of her, lifted off some user's guide or manual instruction, "if they did, my father won't have opted to make these."

"Sorry," Hrth remarked sheepishly, only for her to mumble something to herself thoroughly vexed.

"—it more than blinds," she grumbled as she set herself upon two stiffened hinges that propped the two machines above ground on a platform; a base upon which the machines were firmly welded. It seemed that she'd intended for both hinges to move and then have the platform lower itself into the ground, but the little blonde obviously didn't have that kind of strength in her. The hinges were oxidized and locked stiff, so Hrth assigned himself to the task. After a little while of nothing but standing out there in the storm waiting for Hrth to succeed at it, the little blonde sought for one of the fuel cells in the bag and slapped it hard against the hinges.

"Whoa! Isn't that dangerous? Aren't those power cells or something Pytrice?" Hrth warned and the little blonde gave him the eye. "okay, I won't call you Pytrice," he agreed and let her be. But the winds were getting stronger with the sands eating at their goggles so Hrth bought into the idea and took the bag from her. Requesting the other fuel cell from the twelve year old, he slammed the duo hard against each hinge until one of the hinges buckled. And when it buckled, he smiled, but Pytrice hardly looked impressed. Rather, she looked cognisant of time. He slammed the bag hard against the second hinge and the entire platform actuated itself, robotically lowering the level base beneath the surface, burying both machines beneath the sands into whatever lay beneath.

"Now we can leave," Hrth remarked but Pytrice was already on the move. She didn't even stop—not until they heard a patent cawing under the whirring of the storm. It was a soft sound, seeming to originate from someone with a sore larynx. Pytrice stood dead-still in the storm and so Hrth stopped himself. She activated the gun by uncapping a glass lid. It bleeped then beeped with a steady pulse. Now armed for use.

"Why are we—" he had asked, but she hinted that he remain quiet by pressing a finger against her lips. Her eyes were about the place, darting everywhere and chasing one whir after another. They heard the cawing sound again, so she pointed to the hatch a good distance away. Hrth copied her movements and they backed their way towards the hatch, dead silently.

"What is it?" Hrth whispered the further they got away from the machines but she shoved another finger against her lips, which only set him more on edge, "crawlers?" he inferred and with the look in her eyes, he was spot on right.

"Are they dangerous?" he asked.

"They eat meat," she responded, ever mordacious, but in a very succinct and very gentle whisper; her voice resonating with a feel at variance to the controlled way she handled the gun.

They were now closer to the hatch, but Hrth heard the cawing again. Whatever it was, it sounded closer this time. "You've never used that thing before, have you?" he inferred next. And as the last time, Pytrice's silence was a dead giveaway. He couldn't spot whatever they were to protect themselves from in the obscurity of the storm, but he sure wasn't going to wager his fate on a twelve year old. So Hrth attempted taking the gun from her, but Pytrice won't let him have it.

"No. It will hurt you," she demurred.

"Why?" he demanded.

"If you look at the light when you fire it, it will hurt you," she retorted adamantly, bearing a frown.

"So I should just trust you with this when you've never

even fired the damned thing before?" Hrth whispered back, and she nodded at him requiring he let go of the gun quickly. He was unsure over this course of action but he thought he spotted tears from behind the goggles and was taken aback. "Of what use is having a gun if you can't see what you're firing at?" he rejoined, letting her have the gun just before some kind of creature wandered into their line of sight and Hrth couldn't believe whatever it was his eyes were supposed to be seeing. It appeared to be a naked female with flabby breasts, white, very old, bleached-haired, gaunt and fragile, walking comfortably on all fours, and sniffing the air like a pup. She or it was the freakiest thing he ever saw. If she had eyes, she sure as hell wasn't using them for she had them tightly shut. Unhurriedly yet precisely, she was coming their way. Just she. When they reached the hatch, Pytrice didn't pass the gun or punch in the codes. She only fingered out the executable code across the touchpad for Hrth to key in the combination and unseal the hatch. "pound, pound, hash, zero, pound, one, one," he made a mental note after her, but the moment he chimed in the first key, the supposedly fragile woman charged towards them with sharp teeth, sharp claws, and an even sharper stride. They'd barely been able to crank open the hatch when it lunged at them from a distance. In a fit of desperation, Pytrice triggered the neurolizer with hardly any warning at all. She'd shut her eyes, giving Hrth only a fraction of a window to do same when the pulse hit—still the flash of light that made it through came as a blinding eclipse,

turning his whole world white, silver, and then blank in a matter of seconds.

hoverbot

By the time Hrth came to, and the colours of the world returned to normal, he hadn't noticed he was flat on his back with Pytrice atop him—the little blonde desperately trying to get him to his feet. "Hrth! Get up! Get up!!"

"Where is it?" he demanded on impulse, genuinely not wanting an answer to that question.

"Great! You're okay," she chimed, enthralled he could help himself up, "just get in—quickly! Quickly!"

Pytrice hurried him down the hatch, and was all but in herself, when hard claws clasped around the hatch and suspended her from shutting it. Or going down. The creature's eyes when they opened were whitewashed. They bore no pupils.

"Hrth!" she panicked and Tagho attempted pulling her down the ladder further away from it as it drooled all over them, but it obdurately reached down for Pytrice almost attempting to squeeze its entire body down the hatch. If it could. But its limbs were just too long to get a good grip on the ladder. Or allow it down the slender hatch.

"We need to shut the hatch," she cried.

"No, leave it," Hrth said, "it's not getting in."

"No, we need to shut it," she argued, taking her eyes off the creature for a second, "I'm not going down!" she shot back bravely, but a second too long apparently for it got its chance and pinned her hand to the ladder with its claws.

"Argh! Hrth! Hrth! It has my hand! It has my hand, Hrth!" Pytrice screamed, but her blood and screaming only aggravated the thing, making it ever violent and screaming down the shaft in a raucous boom—an almost deafening noise considering the steel walls of the facility.

"Use the gun! Use the gun!!" Meeko shouted from down the ladder, as the scientist and Haku came to the floor of the hatch. But Pytrice couldn't reach for the plasma neurolizer, neither could Hrth use it, since they had little to no space in the cramped shaft. Nevertheless Hrth held on to her securely, both of them stuck up there and asking Meeko for help.

The scientist was out of his mind with anxiety. "I can't think, Hrth! I can't think," he yelled back, "Just don't let her go—the moment you do, it'll pull her up! It's a carnivore—a meat eater!"

"I know already," Hrth yelled back, spotting the Balinese cat in Meeko's keep.

Pytrice was all tears now, and hurting badly.

"Give me the cat," Hrth demanded from up the ladder, but the very suggestion of it was enough to turn the little blonde against him.

"No! No!" she kneed and shoved against him with the rest of her body, "you leave Kyno out of this!" she decried, her face all flustered and swollen in pain, but her blood dripped into his face.

"She's bleeding, Meeko!"

"Don't ol'pops!" she yelled and Meeko hesitated, "it's just a scratch. Wiggle me out, Hrth! You can wiggle me out!" she demanded. Still at the slightest movement, her wailing was unbearable—even blood came trickling down this time, and once her blood splotched the grounds, it was enough to convince Meeko to hand over the cat.

"Please don't. If you do this I won't forgive you—" she pleaded. A plea that was awkwardly polite and sincere. It made Hrth hesitate before hurling the Balinese cat out of the hatch, and that was all it took; the creature let go almost immediately as the hatch sealed itself automatically, and they fell the full ten feet to the ground.

****

The sturdy hologram table sufficed as a medical bed under such short notice, Pytrice suffering three stabs wounds that bled out her right palm—deep incisions through the dermis pooling in blood as she lay unconscious. Meeko took care of the bleeding. The scientist cast her right hand by spraying empty a canister of QC75 over it—a swift action aerosol from the first aid kit.

"Will she be okay?" Haku asked and Meeko nodded without a word, watching the aerosol cake into a hardened mass.

"You realize you caused this," Hrth spat out, placing the plasma neurolizer upon the table the moment he was certain she was going to be okay. No time for mincing words. "You maliciously put us in harm's way! Why would you send us out knowing those human—things are out there! She's never even fired this before!"

"I would never! This is the first! They don't come out in a storm! Not ever! But I remember telling you to keep her saf—" Meeko responded at first, but interrupting himself to avoid the pitfall of the blame game. "Neither of us have—we've never had to fire any weapon before," he muttered, dolefully watching her lay there, splayed across the table and wounded, "but the gun is a security measure. We carry it for protection."

"Protection?! It almost blindsided me out there." he bellowed at the scientist. "What the hell is it?"

"I'm sorry about that," Meeko apologized, deciding to examine Hrth by the irises, "the gun shoots ionized pulses of white light. The light stuns by blanking out part of your frontal lobes or fully disabling all motor functions through the optic nerve—depending on the intended class of damage to your oblongata."

"Just tell me. Am I okay?" Hrth reacted impatiently.

"But he said he was sorry," Ruke defended the scientist, but this was one conversation he shouldn't have put his mouth in, "it's like he said, those human things are not his fault—"

"Shut up Haku!—I mean Ruke," he spat back, infuriated and demanding more from the scientist than just a petty apology.

"Not humans—crawlers. We call them crawlers—Homo canivarus anomalus, evolved from surviving human populations centuries after the crisis to some particle exposure. They are sentient beings hardly capable of real intelligence," Meeko stated, piecing apart his eye lenses and asking Haku to get some absorbent off the first aid kit and help wipe clean the blood stains across the table.

"Them? There are more of them?" Hrth reacted unkindly to the news, "we're not taking three months of this."

"A world of them, actually. I never told you about them because I didn't think you'd encounter any before you left—particularly in a storm. I thought it was better for your mission if you not know. I realize I was overconfident and I put you all in danger," Meeko apologized but only in tone, and surprisingly, those words stood good enough an apology to Haku.

A sudden thud sent them on edge.

"You need to get me and my brother home as soon as you can," he pointed at Meeko, not even close to forgiving the scientist, before pointing at the bag he'd dropped against the floor. He clocked his head against the wall. "There. What we risked our lives for," he said tastelessly, thoroughly irritated.

Haku separated the bag and fuel cells. Both cells chilled the air and emitted blue illumination. "What are they?" he asked curiously.

"They are power cells. Heavy-duty stuff. We use 'em to power all our machines," Meeko stated, taking the cells from Haku.

Haku was curious. "Are they dangerous?" he asked.

"Same question I asked her before that thing attacked us," Hrth adjoined while attending to his head.

"Quite, but they are well cased so they seldom react," Meeko responded, just before the comm. link went on and highlighted a hint to real time mail. "Watch her and tell me when she wakes, Haku," he requested, pushing down on a button to establish the comm. link.

A female took the screen. She looked of oriental origin to Ruke. "You called Meeko? Got your email, but I think there was something wrong with the hue of your camera. I thought I saw—"

She couldn't believe it, and louder than a banshee she chimed into the speakers, "I don't believe it!"

"Then you are not going to believe what I'm about to tell you," Meeko said, after noticing she'd spotted the two ebony teenagers behind him. "We found them. That's Haku and that's Hrth. They are brothers," the scientist stated proudly and let her face do the speaking. When he thought she'd seen enough, he introduced her to the boys, "this is Lydia. She's in charge at the Alpha Wings. She's a biologist. A real doctor," he praised.

"A molecular biologist. Meeko, isn't that Pytrice on the table?" Lydia asked looking over Meeko's shoulders, and Meeko nodded. "What happened to her?"

"We had a crawler incident only minutes ago, but she's fine."

"Holy Horus!"

"It's still outside. So if you have your shutters down keep them up—keep everyone away from the service hatches," Meeko advised. "If its starves, it might leave."

"I certainly hope so, but it's stormy outside. How come?" she asked.

"I haven't thought it through but I posit our old time-displacement machines must have interrupted one in hibernation. You know they bury themselves anywhere to protect themselves from CME blasts. It's the only reason I can think of. You'll be glad to know that was the very bridge used to transport Haku and Hrth here. It's the silver lining in this whole ordeal. And you'll never guess from what year—"

Pytrice twitched her fingers as slowly as she opened her eyes, and Haku interrupted Meeko. She had a strange look about her so Haku stayed clear of her.

"Feeling at all lightheaded, petridish?" Meeko asked eagerly, placing a palm across her forehead then helping her off the table. She practically weighed a ton for she still had those heavy boots on. Running her boot into Meeko's foot, she shot Hrth a wicked eye as she drew the plasma neurolizer off the table with her good arm.

"Pytrice! Pytrice?" Lydia called from the comm. link, but the little blonde simply limped away with the big gun in hand, ignoring everyone completely.

Haku tried to help the old man to his feet, but Meeko declined, "no. I guess I deserved that. Just hand me that quick cement aerosol," he heaved.

"And what was that about?" Lydia asked from across the comm. link but Meeko hadn't a response for her. He outstretched an arm to Hrth, "I suppose you are the better to apologize to her about losing Kyno," he said, but Hrth baulked at the idea.

"You lost Kyno?—Holy Horus!" Lydia exclaimed from behind the large display screen.

"It was to save her life," the scientist heaved, forcing himself to his feet despite the aching.

"Kyno was David's cat. David was her father. He died in a terrible accident in the labs a year ago," Lydia contributed to help Hrth understand, before stating flatly, "Boys, that cat is the only connection she's felt to David! None of you have a choice in this."

Meeko returned his attention to the comm. link, "she's upset with me."

"I can see that. You should always say something, Meeko. Send her to me if you need my assistance," Lydia advised and Meeko tried on a smile. "So this one's Haku? He's but a kid. I would have gone for the other brother," she remarked as Hrth went by the screen to find Pytrice—wherever the angry blonde hid with a fully operational plasma neurolizer in hand.

****

Hrth found her squatting by the hoverbot, clutching her bleeding palm and trying to put back tears streaking down flushed cheeks. She wiped them off the moment she spotted him coming, and turned away, collapsing her body under the weightless machine. She wasn't in need of company, especially his, and grappled the gun.

"I didn't kn—"

"Don't talk to me!" she growled, cutting him off before his dimwit apology. As he'd guessed, the little blonde was in no mood for talk.

She was lucidly upset and probably volatile at this point, but there was no going back now. He was stuck with her. He just waited patiently, watching her skinny little legs sticking out from under the small bot. It was a peculiarly dense machine for something suspended so effortlessly in the air—and hard as brick too. From the footprints and lettered numbers engraved into its flooring, the bot looked designed for a max of five occupants. Its massive weight bobbed at the slightest touch, in some observable form of equilibrium with the helipad below. Magnets. Probably magnets. The small machine had more bus lines, transistors, and silica chips running its length than the entire history of 20th century technology.

Hrth could stand there forever; Pytrice wasn't going to say a word to him. So he joined her under the machine, slipping beside her. She was visibly irritated and predictably scooted an inch away from him—still not a word.

"I'm sorry for your cat. I didn't know," Hrth apologized after another eternity of silence, then bobbed the hoverbot again, watching the craft dangle effortlessly over them. But Pytrice was content with watching the blast doors a foot away, oblivious to his every gesture, and his very existence.

"I know what it's like. I can't tell you how sorry I am. We lost our father in a car accident barely a week ago," Hrth said softly, but he must have said something to piss her off because before he could let another word slip out of his mouth, Pytrice turned the plasma neurolizer on him. It bleeped. Now armed for use.

"I said don't talk to me!" the twelve year old scowled and Hrth arrested himself as the device beeped with a steady pulse.

He could call her bluff—she wouldn't actually do it?—not if he kept his eyes shut? But, the action alone was enough to buy her some peace and quiet as he watched her for minutes with the gun pointed at him. Hrth lay back down. An inch closer this time. "My brother is scared shitless. But he's all my father left me when he died in that car accident. We both watched him die with our own eyes, can you imagine?" Hrth spoke into oblivion a few minutes later, both of them lost in thought. "I never cried when he died, can you believe that? Almost feels as if something's wrong with me," he confessed, taking another long moment to ponder then deciding to shut up. They lay in silence for more than five minutes, and though it took a while in coming, the gun bleeped after that. This time she'd switched it off. "It's a late reaction," she spoke, better addressing her words to open air.

"A late reaction to what?" he asked tenderly, not looking

her way, so not to be caught between the crosshairs of her emotions. And, she liked it so.

"To his death."

"I see," Hrth answered softly, taking in the moment to really consider all that had happened these last few days.

"Everyone cries," Pytrice said flatly and scooted from under the hoverbot, only to find Meeko and Haku waiting by the craft. She still hadn't forgiven him for murdering her cat if that's what this meant.

˥alpha wings˥

"You were here all along? What took you so long?" Ruke asked his brother same time Pytrice hijacked the questioning, "where are we going, ol'pops?"

The scientist was without his mechanical lenses. "The Alpha Wings. I'm taking Haku and Hrth to meet Lydia," Meeko replied and limped to open the blast doors. He stamped his hand against the biometric scanner and the blast doors leisurely opened up.

Pytrice limped to get her bag but Haku was with the bag already. She noticed she and Meeko both walked with a limp. "Why is he limping?" she asked quizzically.

"He's limping because you kicked him, remember?" Haku retorted in the same mordacious whim she was used to, so she limped to discard the boots and get other stuff.

Needing their help to mount the hoverbot, it bobbed gently when Meeko got on it. Then oscillating tenuously the moment he activated it. This time, with the blast doors wide open, the inlet looked charged somehow, lined with red lights flickering inside it and a white pulse running continuously as far as their eyes can see. "Come on," the scientist reached out his hands to help the boys up the small craft, and they boarded the bot gingerly.

"How many people can travel in this thing?" Haku asked, awed by the craft but Hrth answered him by counting out fingers.

"Just five? How do you know that?" Haku recanted and Hrth fingered at the number of footprints engraved into the bottom of the craft.

"Oh," he breathed sheepishly, "how does it operate?" Haku asked Meeko as the scientist requested they fasten tight peculiar types of restrainers.

"Oscillatory magnetic suspension," Meeko answered, pushing in keys and myriad buttons across the bot's semicircular circuit board.

"What's that?" Haku asked, his mind totally blown away. Pytrice approached with a pair of gloves and another bag in hand. Strangely, she allowed Hrth help her board the craft even as she took her other bag from Haku. "It means it spins to stay in the air," Hrth answered briskly.

Meeko waited for Pytrice to fasten her restrainers.

"What's in there?" Haku asked excitedly but she made up a face. When Meeko looked to her however, she grimaced, "I put in all the empty power cells, okay? We're already headed for the reactor, aren't we?" she shot at him.

Meeko tugged against a lever and the hoverbot sailed effortlessly into the inlet. It swayed and swerved slowly according to its path down the long channel; too slowly in fact that Haku took off his restrainer, "it's slower than I expected. I can match this thing if I get off," he commented and Pytrice humphed.

"You wouldn't want to do that," Meeko advised, "this channel is one big electromagnet. Once activated, the panels," Meeko pointed at the walls, "become electrified and keep the bot in potential difference with the ramps," he pointed out the ledges and buttresses supporting the flickering lights, "the p.d. is what makes the bot glide so smoothly. It's very dangerous." Now the scientist turned an eye to Hrth, "as with sleeping under the bot. Once operational, this bot creates a PD with the ground. The magnetic core it forms can dent an iron plate. It's dangerous, Hrth. You shouldn't sleep on the launch pad."

"I hadn't known. She was—" Hrth responded before interrupting himself, watching colour suffice Pytrice's cheeks and a smug grin appear on her face, "you know you have to tell her that. You know that, don't you?" he reported.

"Pytrice? I have warned her countless times. She just likes to have it her way," Meeko stated.

"I don't feel it spinning. If it spins to move, why isn't it spinning now?" Haku asked, only for Hrth to wave his brother off.

"enough of the questions, Ruke. You shouldn't even ask that," Hrth snapped, feeling the vibrations beneath their feet.

"Oh no don't stop him. Yes he should! His curiosity is what makes me sure he's Haku, and you're you, Hrth," Meeko butt in.

The brothers were confused.

"Are you saying this Haku and Hrth myth could be

anyone of us?" the early teen was beginning to ask when Meeko cut in again.

"No, no, no. You're Haku and he's Hrth!" Meeko affirmed.

"Why?" Hrth retorted.

"—is it because you say so?" Haku asked simply and Meeko found himself stuttering.

"No, no, no! You're Haku because you want to know. You need to know! He's Hrth because not only is he your brother, he wants to protect you. He always wants to protect you. He'd give his life for you if it comes to that," Meeko retorted, flustered and red, so both brothers let it rest.

"Listen. There are two magnetic gyrostats spinning inside this bot, Haku—" Meeko had begun explaining when Pytrice pushed on the lever to the max, exasperated with all their talking, so the bot ran the entire length to the Alpha Wings, covering an approximate one and a half mile in less than a minute. To all with their restrainers attached, the lights passed in a blur. Not much could be said for the boy without the restraint though.

****

New Alert: Incoming transport detected.

On getting the alert, Lydia pushed the safety button and left the control port. The blast doors opened up and the hoverbot came in to a soft landing. The doctor stood taller than anyone Haku had ever seen. She was standing by the landing pad waiting for the bot to dock.

"Seal the doors," she said to a boy half her height who'd been standing beside her, and the child trudged sickly to go stick his hand against a biometric scanner.

"And who's that?" Haku asked concernedly when the blast doors shut behind them.

"That's Myk. Lydia's son. He suffers from autism, so try not to mention it," Meeko responded swiftly as the bot came to a halt.

"Boys!" Lydia greeted warmly as the two ebony teenagers and the old scientist came off the bobbing bot. Pytrice chose to debark absent anyone's aid. There was someone a yard away working the control port. "Tee Wyr, come say hello," she announced animatedly, and took their hands. Her son returned, looking sombre and unexcited, but she took time to reintroduce the strangers and offered Myk's hand mechanically. "He's fifteen," Lydia said proudly, with good reason for Myk was taller than Haku and almost as tall as Hrth. He had short auburn hair.

"And tall! I have Asperger's syndrome! I eat welt wheat on F—"

Lydia placed a hand on Myk's shoulder and whispered something in his ear; something bizarre because he suddenly shut it and grew very quiet counting his fingers.

"It's true he's tall," Haku commented and she chortled. Tee Wyr came down from the port and he was about the height of Hrth, but he looked older with rich hair, a faint beard, was a shade too light to be Asian, and apparently, a friend of Pytrice. She lifted her other working palm at him and they slapped hands, "what's putretfying buzzkill!" they hailed and Pytrice opened her bag, "got you a treat," she teased and unloaded her bag of spent cells. He chuckled.

"What's with the cast arm?" Tee Wyr asked and she walked off.

"You can ask them," she retorted, heading for the elevated control port; globular in design.

"You have to let me take a good look at that hand, Pytrice," Lydia interjected.

"Just leave it alone, Lydia. I'm fine," the little blonde snapped.

"You should always say something when you're hurt!" Lydia yelled after her and followed her up as Tee Wyr offered a hand to both visitors.

"This is Tee Wyr. He's like the communications techie here at the Alpha Wings," Meeko introduced.

Tee Wyr was lucidly fascinated by the feel of their skin. "It doesn't feel leathery," he observed. "So sorry, this is a new experience for me. I was told your kind was extinct since the Reanimation Era—"

"And they are," Meeko interjected smugly, "they travelled through a time bridge to get here."

Tee Wyr's eyes lit up like flares, "No way old man! How many years back?"

"Over a million," Meeko stated proudly and the rich haired dude whistled.

"Buzzkill!"

They all convened at the control port.

"This place is much bigger than your space," Hrth commented, watching a large concave structure far up in the ceiling above their heads.

"And with good reason, this is the observatory," Meeko explained, "what you're looking at is a sky lens. We use it to see into orbit and shoot free to air signals into the ionosphere."

"Is that the dome we saw from far out?" Haku asked and Meeko nodded.

"Yes. Roughly about two and half kilometres away," Meeko agreed then requested Lydia show it to them. She triggered the shutters and a flood of light illuminated the entire place. Somehow it made the place feel hotter. "the lenses have a high refractive index. When the shutters are down, Tee Wyr uses it to shoot signals to other facilities like ours. He shuts the shutters when we're done."

The world looked like a sand and clay desert, dead and starved of life. The heavens, on the other hand, looked wholly different and peaceful. It had cirrus clouds of brown colouring and some pink teal streamers animating the heavens. But there, poised in place behind it all, stood two suns and an arched moon.

"That's Ra," Meeko stated, pointing to the bigger and far less bright of the celestial bodies, "while that's Horus. The troublesome one," he stated pointing to the smaller brightly burning sun.

The brothers were blown away. "I don't believe it," Hrth garbled.

"Buzzkill! I never thought I'd hear someone say that of the suns—," Tee Wyr chuckled, finding it hard to believe the expressions slouched on their faces.

"Horus is responsible for killing almost everything. Many cells aren't built to stand a lot of irradiation no matter how evolved," Lydia interrupted, while forcing an inspection into the blonde's arm.

"If the sun's so dangerous, how come the thing that caused that is still out there?" Hrth recanted, referring to Pytrice's arm. Lydia interrupted Meeko from answering; she was taken by his candour.

"Somehow I recall speaking about most cells, Hrth," she iterated to be specific, —crawlers have a different physiology."

"Holy Horus! You got that from a crawler and you kept shut?" Tee Wyr exclaimed and the blonde walled off her eyes.

Lydia wasn't done speaking, "their somatic cells have a loose range for radiation tolerance, but even for living cells there's a limit to how much amount they tolerate because radiation causes decay. It's why they age very quickly. Crawlers seldom stay out in the open for long. Which is also why they have to hibernate in the shade."

"yes, but only during high coronal mass ejection pleiades," Meeko interjected to further her explanation, whatever that meant. "—it's when Horus burns through everything," he said to elucidate even further. "The crawler that attacked Pytrice should be about 16-17 years of age."

"You mean the old woman?" Hrth asked.

"She does look like an old woman, doesn't she?"

"The moon's out there. Why's the moon out there?" Haku asked and Tee Wyr opted to reply.

"that's the way it is. It's always been out there."

"No, the moon's supposed to come out at night?" Haku argued.

"What night?—you guys are definitely not from around here," Tee Wyr laughed, "the moon's always out and the sun's always up. There is no night."

"What?"

"The celestial bodies are no longer at the positions you grew up knowing," Meeko explained and Pytrice hopped off the control port immediately Lydia was done with the forced inspection of her cast.

"I'm off to the reactors," she blurted out to whomever it may concern, in some way seeking some self-imposed solitude and hoping Lydia would get the point. And Lydia did get the point, in Lydia's own special way that is. "Myk, go with her," Lydia instructed and the fifteen year old got up mechanically and headed to a huge automated door well before the little blonde could finish a tantrum. She didn't look pleased with the oriental woman.

"Did you have to invite the knucklehead?"

"Don't call him that," Lydia shot back.

Tee Wyr jumped into the fray deciding to help Pytrice with the spent fuel cells, "I think i should give our newcomers a tour of the premises, if it's okay by you guys?" he requested and Lydia and Meeko grabbed at the opportunity he afforded them, so Pytrice turned her frown on Tee Wyr.

"Suck it up buzzkill, you're with us," he frowned back. He wasn't buying her act. Besides, it was obvious to him that Meeko and Lydia needed a little privacy—some good time alone together as he led the troop after Myk.

****

It took a while in coming. It was not like Lydia to be quiet. if he knew Lydia the way he knew Lydia, she was bound to be all at him in a short moment—if she really liked the boys that is. Or had an inkling of belief any of this was at all possible.

"All I see are two simple kids, Meeko. What are you trying to achieve with this?" she asked eventually, and pointedly.

"Same thing you're trying to achieve with Pytrice," the old scientist replied succinctly, walking to a circuit board and resurrecting a diagnostic hologram of the galactic universe.

"And what would that be?" she pressed, "you hardly look the role playing stepmom—"

"No, but helping her survive—that's what you do,"

Meeko answered softly, then pointing Lydia to the Haematic star system, "this is it," he said candidly to her, "the best planetary system with a young star. All planets in the least sit 54% water with a 20 mile ring of breathable gas and nitrogen—25% of which is O2 and O3 ionized. It's more than we need to survive." The physicist rubbed his hands in excitement.

"You know that's a long shot," she said to him before powering down the hologram and the sky lens above.

"I know that," he conceded, "but there is a first time for a man of science to have a little faith. Haku and Hrth made it this far, didn't they?"

"And what's makes you so certain they are Haku and Hrth?" she asked gently, a soft smile growing on her face.

"You want a textbook reason or my own reason?" the old man asked and Lydia finally let out a laugh. She'd bought into it.

"Give me your reason," she requested tenderly, "for the moment that you're a man of faith."

"The younger kid is knowledge hungry and wilfully present. I'm sure he's going to be heard. I can feel it in this old heart," Meeko said, "while the other one, the older brother, he's always so protective—so uptight. You've witnessed it yourself. I am telling the truth, am I not?" he asked her plainly. "Besides, we have no other options. We're already dying out in more ways than one. You of all know best that is not an index of speech."

Lydia held Meeko by the shoulders and settled the scientist into a comfy chair with leg rests, "so what's your other reason?" she asked and sat beside him.

He didn't seem too comfortable sharing the secret with her, but that was just a tease, "They have Rostov's Persephone. Rostov found a way, I haven't figured how yet, to beat scale mechanics and propel Persephone before the sun goes schism. He succeeded by just a few years. So, in a manner of speaking, those two boys are from the future—our future."

Lydia couldn't remain seated.

"We search for Persephone as we speak," Meeko stated and she was blown away.

"Do they know about the prophecy then? Have you told them?" she inquired sincerely.

"They already know," Meeko answered, and more than generously.

"They're kids. No one's that straightforward with kids. Have you told them, Meeko?" she asked again, a questionable mow creeping up her face, "you do know what I'm talking about. The prophecy implicitly says only one will make it back home and we both know who that is."

"No one has to die," Meeko argued uneasily, a pensive brow breaking his countenance. "All we have to be is careful, Lydia, and we'll make up our future—because that's what the future is. We make up our own reality."

"All the versions say the very same thing so it'll be better they find out from you than someone else, Meeko. All the same, I think we should keep their presence strictly limited to the facility," Lydia suggested and the scientist agreed; this juncture, now in time, being a fragile moment in the making.

solar flare

Contrary to what the brothers had expected, the reactor room was frigid and had frozen foam icing up working cylinders. Haku lifted his fingers to touch, but Tee Wyr stopped him. "Don't touch that," he warned.

"Why? It's going to hurt me, isn't it?" Haku asked, catching everyone's attention. Everyone but Myk.

"No," Pytrice rejoined in her typically mordacious whim. Tagho chuckled but Ruke ignored them both.

"That's frozen nitrogen. Not good," Tee Wyr warned, showing off a fraction of his palm blackened to frostbite. The younger brother kept his fingers to himself. Myk led the way past the cryogenic cylinders, up iron staircases and round a humongous concentric dish to where an open board of ports was waiting. Pytrice grabbed the bag of cells from Tee Wyr as she headed for the board. "So are you the only ones here?" Haku asked.

"See anyone else?"she rejoined again shoving the autistic kid rudely aside.

"There was a time we made 25," Tee Wyr answered sadly, "but that was a long time ago. Our gene pool's been on a decline ever since."

"25 hundred or 25 thousand?" Hrth asked, evaluating the sheer size of the facility.

"No way," Tee Wyr scoffed, "Just 25, but other facilities we hear have a formidable populace. Like the remote islands, they say they count a whopping 50."

"What's 50? Fifty's fifty? 50 means you're dying," Hrth said morbidly.

Tee Wyr took a long look at Pytrice's cast arm as she fit and slammed each cell into a free port across the board to charge, "we needn't thank the crawlers for that. You can take the cast off, Pytrice," he suggested and the little blonde cracked the cast against an iron bar and tore it off for it'd been making her uncomfortable. Her palm looked good as new, save the scarring incurred, so she slapped on some hand gloves. It still hurt though, from the way she worked her fingers. The blue lights lit up on the cells when she plugged them in and they recharged automatically.

"If you've lived here so long, why haven't you filled up this space?" Haku inquired and Tee Wyr returned a warm smile.

"It's not that easy, inbreeding makes a species more susceptible to disease. And we've had a lot of that around here. Despite that, Meeko makes an unsuitable mate. He doesn't admit it, but the problem's not his age. He can't produce a fertile offspring, a frequent happening when the world you contact is radiated. Ever since we lost Da—" Tee Wyr opted to skip the words for the sake of arousing the wrong emotions, "Meeko and Lydia don't make a match. I and Lydia don't make a match—that would be weird. The only match now is her and him," he stated and Haku marvelled at the idea of the stubborn blonde pairing up with the autistic pushover. "Besides, Meeko says we stumble upon distress signals of crawlers overrunning the facilities once or twice a decade so we'll probably die out long before they get here—and that's good news."

"You call that good news?" Haku retorted.

"Over being eaten alive?—of course!" Tee Wyr answered, "remind me to show you one of my gismos when we return to the control port. Crawlers evolved from us and I'm of the opinion they are smarter than they look, contrary to what Lydia and Meeko think. So, I've been shooting my own sonar signals into the air. 'kind of goes like this—tin tan tang tan thang! tin tan tang tan thang!!"

"What's it mean?" Haku asked enamoured by the tune Tee Wyr was desperately trying to make.

"it's a rhythm of aural notes—you can call it some kind of subliminal mathematical advertisement," Tee Wyr interpreted with a smug and silly smile about his face, "it'll be my way of saying We Are Your Mother—so don't eat us," he said and Haku found it funny.

"I see why Meeko is desperate for prophecy," Hrth confessed beneath a snort, but then there was this odd silence. Tee Wyr looked to Pytrice but she didn't say anything.

"No way! So you and old Meeko were just going to keep me out of the loop like some dummy, weren't you?" Tee Wyr asked, apparently offended by something even as Pytrice proceeded to pop off the cells that had charged themselves full from the charging ports.

"Ol'pops thinks they are Haku and Hrth, not me," she

answered without hesitation or compunction, bagging up the cells. "It's none of my biz."

"if that's the prophecy of the surrogate reality, you don't mind if it gets us all killed?" Tee Wyr retorted when the CME warning hit. It was a recurring wailing sound and the power in the room waned ominously. The autistic kid lost his temporal platitude. "CME! cMe! CME! cMe!" he yelped repeatedly and jarringly, almost as though the blaring alarm hadn't sufficed in racking their ears. Immediately, he bolted for safety through the greenhouse route. Both Tee Wyr and Pytrice's eyes were all about the place as each working cylinder in the reactor room slowly ground to a rhythmic halt.

"What's a CME?" Hrth asked anxiously, but there wasn't any time to respond. Pytrice abandoned the fuel cells and jolted for the observatory with Hrth on her heels, but Tee Wyr demurred to going back that route, "we wouldn't make it in time! Myk's right! Follow Myk! Greenhouse 15 seconds!!" he yelled on noticing the autistic boy genius heading in a beeline the other way.

"Forget the knucklehead! We can't wait for the bot," Pytrice objected.

"we don't have to—we'll make it by foot," Tee Wyr yelled back and straight away she changed direction.

"Pick up the charged cells! They can't be outside," he advised but Hrth opted to yank all the cells out of charging and toss them in the bag. It made a ton of weight, but Tee Wyr helped with the other end of the bag as they all raced the opposite direction towards another blast door overshadowed by a flight of stairs.

The voices of Meeko and Lydia forced their way through the PA broadcast and fluctuating power supply, "Get o—there n—ow. Solar—fla—minent," but that just was barely enough a warning when the PA system died. Pytrice scurried past the boys and jumped the flight of steps to make it in time to where the second blast door was concealed, slapping her hurting palm against its bioscanner. It lit green and barely lifted itself off the floor when the light, air and power systems went out and the reactor room flashed a crimson red.

"Is it open?" Tee Wyr asked and she nodded, being the first to squeeze her way into the tunnel.

"I mean did you override the destination door?" he rephrased and she answered impatiently, "Yes! I said yes!"

"I'm not getting in there. It's powered," Haku reacted on spotting similar flashing bands of red light inside the tunnel, "then wait and see what's coming," Pytrice snorted hastily. Tee Wyr and Hrth helped Myk through the blast door, as well as slip the bags through the barely sufficient opening. "Com'on Ruke! It's not powered," Hrth demanded hastily but grabbed his brother into the electromagnetic tunnel when a countdown sequence initiated. They all had 25 seconds to get to the greenhouse.

"What's a CME? And why is it counting down?" Hrth asked, as they skipped the buttresses and avoided the ledges down the tunnel.

"Solar flare—it's when Horus burns through everything," Tee Wyr answered, breathing heavily, and recommending the brothers do the same.

"if it burns through everything, why are we headed for the greenhouse?" Haku asked, a heel behind Pytrice, when he noticed what seemed to be an iridescent wall coming down the end of the tunnel and coming for them. "What is that?!" he asked anxiously.

"The greenhouse is magnet and particle insulated to keep the greens in stable condition—and that's the first of the heat wave so hurry. It's coming."

Pytrice sprung herself through the other blast door which fortunately had had a 20 second window override to open halfway before the power went out, so getting into the greenhouse chamber was relatively easy. She anxiously sought to help Haku in. Tee Wyr and Hrth tossed the bag of fuel cells into the greenhouse when they noticed they were one person short—Myk! The autistic kid was having a seizure down the tunnel. Hrth had about a tenth of a minute to decide his fate as well as Myk's. So he counted each second in the 7-second window left to get Myk safely within the confines of the greenhouse. The iridescent wall revealed itself to be a viridescent wall of fire, burning off the metallic element lining the tunnel and atomizing every free organic molecule upon contact with it. It wasn't the only wall of fire that passed though. And only after each wall of fire had passed, did the light and power flick back on.

****

Meeko and Lydia had locked themselves somewhere around the observatory. When everything came online, the entire facility even the air had distilled itself. Not a speck of dirt was in sight.

"That's the second in three days. Something's not right," Lydia whispered as Meeko made his way back to the control port, limping all the way. He activated the PA broadcast as well as the sky lens above and there it was, keeping the shutters from opening all the way—it'd also chinked the glass by a crack which was not good.

"You may very well be right about that," Meeko answered on noticing the charred impression of what was once a crawler against the sky lens.

"is that the one that hurt—?"

"I suppose so."

"How in the world—was it trying to get in?" she asked anxiously and the old man objected calmly.

"probably found nowhere to hide."

"hopefully there are no others out there. It's been forever since our last builder."

"It's what has me puzzled," Meeko said and took the PA to broadcast. "Is everyone alright? Is Haku and Hrth still with you?" he inquired, waiting for a response behind the static.

"The whole place is caving in. I pray you're right about that prophecy," Lydia muttered morosely watching the chinked glass.

Haku had slipped trying to get into the greenhouse, luckily Pytrice yanked him into safety. Hrth, on the other hand, now had his fingers caught between Myk's teeth. Myk had been foaming from the mouth and it'd taken Tee Wyr a gruelling 20-seconds to pry Hrth's hand free of those strong alligator-like jaws. It was a grim sight.

"You're a hero, Hrth. Thank you. Lydia is practically going to kiss you for saving his life," Tee Wyr said to Hrth as Myk lay steady across the floor, his system normalized.

"Is he always like this?" Hrth asked, trying to clamp down on the pain pulsing through his wrist by stretching and massaging both hands when the PA system went on and a video of the physicist and biologist came up on one of the display screens by the door handle.

"Is everyone alright?" Meeko had asked on noticing the five individuals exhausted and flat against their backs, with Myk recovering from his epileptic fit.

"Myk! Myk!" Lydia called from behind.

"He's alright. He had a fit just when the CME warning hit but Hrth saved him. He risked his life, but he saved him!" Tee Wyr mentioned gently and Lydia's face flooded with emotion.

"Thank you, Hrth. We're grateful," Meeko summed up for her in a few words but Hrth wouldn't reply the scientist. There was this look in the elder teen's eye, and since Meeko knew he'd have to deal with it later, he sought to change focus, "that's enough touring for today, I think. You should head back. Where are you guys?"

"The greenhouse," Pytrice replied, shoving Haku off her breasts to rise to her feet.

"Hey," he protested as he butt into his brother who head-butt Tee Wyr in the process.

"Get here as soon as you can. We'll activate the hoverbot to come pick you up," he said. "And thank you again Hrth...eh..for...saving him," he uttered before quickly killing the comm. link.

Pytrice deliberately shoved past them and pressed her hand against the bioscanner to open the way into the greenhouse. As expected of greenhouse gases, the darkened chamber was even hotter than the arid lands above ground. Only this time, an oppressive dampness of moisture and humidity imbued the air, making it quite difficult to sweat in there despite the heat. The plants in the greenhouse didn't look like real plants either; with their fluorescent colours of pink, teal green and purple, much in the same way they looked any closer to real people under the unreal lighting and shadows about the room.

"Are they alien?" Ruke inquired, awed by the esoteric beauty of all the plants growing in open or airtight bouquets of dirt or clear water. The massive chamber looked so delicate with the seedlings separated by age and grade and aisles, all the way from the right hand of the room to the full grown shrubs to the left of the room.

"No, they aren't," Tee Wyr replied.

"But it looks so alien. These are not the type we're used to seeing at green earth," Haku remarked about the plants.

"Actually they are, even if they are genetically modified. That's what our archives tell us," Tee Wyr disagreed politely. "We've been doing this for years. it's how we survived."

"No, these are not the plants we have back home. I recognize some of their shapes but this fruit—besides, our plants are green, you know? As in green earth," Ruke argued, dragging out the conversation for longevity.

"Rukewe, don't argue with him," Tagho cut in, tapping his brother across the nape but this time, Haku shoved him away angrily.

"Why do you do that? Stop doing that! I hate that!" he barked at the much older brother, catching Pytrice's attention who'd intended to open up the main doors and lead them out. This was to be interesting.

"Don't you see it's the lights? Why do you like asking silly questions when you'll discover the answer if you just take a moment to look around? They are UV lights."

"yes we use UV and Near Red lights to cultivate our organic food. The blasts outside would kill them but inside here, to these artificial lights—white light's only a waste of energy," Tee Wyr cut in as though it would do any good, but the fight only got worse.

"All you had to do was say that in the first place without slapping my head!" Ruke retorted, shoving his brother again and belligerently, closer and ever closer to the delicate bouquets. "And these are my questions, not yours. If I choose ask them then back off. Besides, I'm the important one! Not you! I fell and you didn't even save me. You're supposed to save me, but you didn't—" Ruke let out like a steaming kettle but interrupted himself, catching on quickly before he caused any more damage as his words had fallen like the bomb that eviscerated Hiroshima once in a million lifetimes ago. There was a change in the older one's countenance, but Hrth felt betrayed and hurt in more ways than he had realized at that moment.

Pytrice put a hand to her face as one whole bouquet crashed to the ground and jolted autistic Myk from his temporary platitude. "I'm the important one! Important meaning worthy of note or consideration than the other! Haku's the important one!" he uttered without end. And with no one to shut him up.

"What do you mean by that?" Tagho demanded immediately and Ruke had no answer, unsure if this would be the day his brother would lay a hand on him. Regrettably with Pytrice watching. He turned around and wouldn't, or couldn't, say a word even as Tagho held him sternly by the shoulder and pit two glazed NR blackened eyes against him, "who told you that?"

Tee Wyr tried speaking for the younger one, easy to pick up on the fact a fight in the greenhouse would not turn up pleasant for anyone, but Hrth wouldn't even listen to him so he hurriedly moved to rescue the dying plant the brothers had knocked over and placed it in a spare bouquet. It was the welt wheat plant, a smelly kind of oat when microwaved. Autistic Myk was unable to get the phrase 'important one' out of his head; plus the chanting drove Tagho crazy. "Will you tell him to shut up!" Tagho demanded off Pytrice but the independent twelve year old didn't bother to do as required. She just opened up the blast doors and proceeded to the port, since it was more than obvious they had no intention of pulverising each other. They could meet there whenever they were done bickering.

"Rukewe who told you that?"

Hrth wouldn't go without an answer, so he turned to Tee Wyr the moment the young man with dirt and gloves in hand was done fixing up their damage. "What did you mean by what you said before?"

"What did i say?" Tee Wyr parried.

"Don't start. What did you mean by a prophecy's that's going to get us all killed? You said that before didn't you?"

Tee Wyr couldn't tell what kind of answer Hrth was looking for or what would relieve him from the venom coursing through his blood. There was actually venom in his blood from a variant of the poison oak Hrth had knocked over. It would take a minute or two for the poison to kick in. "I'm not so sure anymore. I was only wondering how he'll beat the scale mechanics. Something Meeko once took seriously in our earlier days when he didn't believe in prophesies. Now I'm thinking it's nothing of note since he's not said anything," he tried to excuse himself.

"what scale mechanics?"

"Again it's just Meeko, Hrth, so if you do want to know—truthfully, only Meeko can explain it to you the best way how," he answered sheepishly.

"Don't call me, Hrth!" Hrth roared before turning to his brother, "it's Meeko isn't it? He's been filling your head with these dreams of a saviour, hasn't he?"

Ruke quietly and remorsefully shoved off his brother's grip as the hoverbot came into port. Myk was still parroting on like a broken CD when they boarded the bot, "Meeko's theorem of scale mechanics: no material in any given universe can be protracted to a time before it was conceived. No energy in a closed system can be abridged to a value lower than its true value at any given point in time—"

"Is he going to quit his yapping, or should I shut him up?" Tagho demanded off the cuff, livid as a wasp, so Tee Wyr put a hand to Myk's lips, whispering something else into his ears as a detour to his thoughts and to actively engage Myk's mind. It was the only way to quiet the autistic savant from inflicting further discomfort. "If you're sincerely grateful for me saving his life, you will let me know what Meeko isn't telling me," he said as a tautening rash developed along his arm and hardened into ridges. The rash didn't stay for long though. It was only poisoned oak.

scale mechanics

There was that inimitable glaze in Hrth's black eyes ever since the five came off the hoverbot, even after they yielded to light banter over the harrowing experience of surviving the life threatening ordeal and back.

Lydia was all over them and Pytrice as usual didn't find her doting any more pleasant. "I'm fine. Can you stop touching me now?" she spoke brusquely as she brushed by, heading for cryogenics and probably someplace to be away from all the yapping over the extremely ordinary experience. She lifted her healed palm to Meeko's inquisitive eyes as she ambled by, not wanting him to step in her way. Or interrupt her.

Lydia turned her attention to the brothers and Myk. "Thank you for rescuing him," she said with a broad smile and Haku smiled back. When Hrth returned her smile however, his was big, broad, and fake. The elder teen had more on his mind. He had Meeko on his mind. And Lydia could see that. So after inspecting his arm, she turned to her little savant and let him have his space.

"Where's she headed?" Haku asked watching Pytrice disappear behind some door and Tee Wyr took him by the hands in response.

"Cryo," he replied without any concern before announcing into one ear, "come with me to the control port. I want to show you those signals."

"great!" Ruke stated, leaving with Tee Wyr for a more

private compartment at the centre of the observatory. Another compartment, one made and sealed off with glass.

There was a light in the younger one's eyes like a lithium flashlight. That flashlight was probably the reason why the elder teen hadn't broached his grievance, yet. In any way, and no matter how long it took to beat around the bush, Meeko realized there was no better time to square with the truth than now. He gave Hrth the acknowledgement he'd been waiting for, but only after Haku disappeared from the observatory and was outside earshot. Almost literally, their words bumped into each other, "I know what you're not telling me—I have something to tell you."

"go ahead," they said to each other in unison after that, still Hrth was impatient to speak his mind.

"From the first time we got here, I knew it. I knew there was something you were not telling me."

"Hrth—"

"Don't call me that!" Tagho shot back. "I don't know what you're trying to pull but I do not appreciate you getting between my brother and I! He's susceptible to all you tell him because we've lost everything, but don't for one second think I'd sit by and watch you make a pawn out of him to whatever game it is you're playing here," he spoke angrily, directing his finger not only at Meeko but Lydia as well.

"Point taken," Meeko admitted too quickly for him to be listening.

"You're not listening to me! Just like when I said I wanted you to get us back home!" he boomed at Meeko, luckily the glass compartment was totally sealed off and so no one else heard his voice.

"You're not listening to me! You're not listening to me! You're not listening to me!"

Lydia whispered a word in Myk's ear and the mind parroting robot stirred himself to someplace god knows where. "I know you're upset," Lydia interrupted very gently, "and you have every right to be, but you must believe me, you must take my word for it if not Meeko's; we have every intention of getting you back home as quickly as we can. We mean you or your brother no harm; even if Meeko comes across as desperate. Please?" Hrth took a deep breath to get a grip on his anger, so she turned to Meeko, "now will be a good time to tell him," she admitted.

"I'm not going to tell him what's not true," Meeko replied stubbornly, putting a hand to his temples as though he'd just caught a migraine.

"But you said you would?"

"I know what i said Lydia, you needn't remind me over and over," he spat at her.

"If you don't tell him Meeko, then I will," Lydia shot back.

"I already know," Tagho interrupted tired of watching them bicker. "We're all going to die. That is your high-sounding prophesy isn't it?"

"What makes you say that?"

"Your operator! According to him, you're above your head with this surrogate reality you're prattling on about. He said you told him that yourself at a time when you were your more rational self," Hrth stated emphatically and both Meeko and Lydia for a brief moment set their focus on the two prattling birds in high spirits inside the more private glass compartment a good distance away.

"He's wrong," Meeko rejoined though it sounded more a confession of faith.

"You mean you are wrong? Are we to disappear in your egotistical venture into time? Or didn't you ever say the physics of attempting such a thing goes against the laws of the universe? Didn't you? Or would you rather I quote you verbatim?—all practical applications of it lead to zero—the time continuum can be relied upon to undo what is done if at all it was infinitesimally possible!"

Meeko butt in, "that was until Persephone. that was until Rostov changed everything."

"But it was you who postulated that? Wasn't it you?" Hrth demanded. "Unlike what you think about me, I listen Meeko."

"I was young then. Nothing more than a prattling fool."

Hrth chuckled in sarcasm, "that was you a week ago, Meeko," he snarled. "Tee Wyr told me everything."

"He doesn't know Rostov beat the scale. You'll just have to believe me when I say I can get you—and I will get you and your brother safely home."

Out of concern Lydia was about to take back that promise, but Meeko halted her mid-tense.

"How? You are not Rostov. You don't even know how to get us back Mr. Scientist."

"I admit I don't know, but i believe i have now what is required."

"What is that?" Hrth sneered.

"Belief. I believe now as Rostov did. Your being here makes all the difference. Give me these three months then you can call me a liar."

"And is your faith supposed to get us home? Or are you ready to forfeit all our lives just to prove yourself?"

"Our world is dying, Hrth. It's already forfeit if I don't do something," Meeko stated flatly with what seemed to be tears pooling just beneath the scientist's defiant eyes, so Lydia took the Meeko by the hand to comfort him.

"You must know it's a sacrifice we all will gladly make to save this world, Hrth," she pronounced softly and caught the late teen dumbfounded.

****

The wavelengths displayed across the display screens in the small glass compartment were sinusoidal at first, then after a recorded silence or flat of 6 seconds, superimposed themselves in amplified frequencies; all of similar rhythmic curves. This was Tee Wyr's sonar signal.

"it looks complicated. you think the crawlers can make sense of this."

"if at all they respond to sound I don't see why not? Lydia suspects they use it in recreating their environment," he said, offering to share with Haku two transparent and cordless earphones to help listen to the symphonic pulses.

"What 'you mean by that?" Haku replied inserting the right earphone into his left ear and snapping his fingers to as many pulses as he could hear.

"She says they see through hearing, which is why they can sense us by just listening."

"You mean like echolocation?"

"Yeah, echolocation," he parroted excitedly, "but even better than that. They can sense colours through listening the way we see colours through seeing! How cool is that?!"

"Pretty cool, I guess. I think i can make out your rhyme now; we are your Mother, we are your mother, but the pulses come really fast," Haku remarked, having meant that to be a compliment even as Tee Wyr held up a smug grin. "What? What is it?" he quizzed.

"You hear it as sonic pulses, but if you were a crawler you'd hear my rhyme way differently," Tee Wyr answered and watched with smug excitement Haku eyes light up the moment he demodulated the superimposed frequencies so the signals came through the computer as pure orchestral magic. He was so proud, he bypassed the earphones and channelled the output through some speakers. "I believe this music might come in handy if one of them ever finds its way down here."

"I don't doubt it will," Haku replied awed by the melody. "It more than a jingle, Tee Wyr. It's very complex."

"I know. Cool, isn't it?"

"Very cool," Haku said and held up a knuckle.

"What's that?"

"We rub knuckles. It's what we do back home. Just rub knuckles," he instructed and Tee Wyr did.

"Buzzkill," they both said with the same breath.

"Is it true what you said to my brother on the bot?" Haku asked after a while and around the time Myk burst in. "Do you think it is impossible for Meeko to send us back?"

"I don't know. I told your brother what he wanted to hear because he pressed me too."

"Do you really believe we're all going to die then? I don't want to die."

"I don't know," Tee Wyr answered but Haku's question had been ambiguous and loud enough to jolt Myk from his temporary platitude.

"Everything dies that is not a complex number! Everything dies that is not a sine function!" Myk retorted and chanted over and over on meeting the question and the number of wavelengths across the screens.

"Thank you for summing that up," Tee Wyr cheered light -heartedly and whispered a tailored question into Myk's ear to steer the savant towards the value of pi and its decimals; much away from such a grim subject.

****

Cryogenics stood an endless chamber from through its glass window. Like their lodging, the entrance to the chamber was a rotating cylinder and Hrth could spot Pytrice through the glass as well as the dozens in her company. So when the cylinder rotated and he stepped in, he'd intended to keep his silence. Not until he realized it was no ordinary chamber.

"Are those bodies?" he asked, watching her stand by some kind of capsule with yellow light emanating from its inside. She was starring down at the lifeless body inhabiting it. A body frozen over and still with time, notwithstanding the innumerable number of similar capsules lining the chamber as far as the eye could see. Pytrice was reticent to reply. "they are people," she shot back.

"dead people?" he asked, but took her silence as meaning yes. He drew close to her and waited by her chosen capsule with a reserved countenance. "So this is what he looks like? He looks like you, only stronger," he muttered to tease her into conversation, but was content with the brittle smile she threw his way when she looked at him.

"He's frozen," Pytrice muttered back. "It makes him look stronger."

"I see," Hrth said, looking around the room. The air in the chamber felt a fraction cooler and cleaner than anywhere else he'd been since he arrived, so he asked her when he noticed her tone warm up a degree, "what happened to him? If you can tell me, I'd like to know?"

Hrth had asked softly but for a moment there he'd thought he seen a tear trickle down her cheeks and almost concluded he'd pushed too hard when she answered, "it was an accident. We were busy making adjustments to the neurolizer in Tech lab. He'd told me to fetch Tee Wyr but when i came back, there he was— lying on his back like he's lying now. He didn't even notice me. Couldn't recognize me," she explained, not able to shear her eyes off his corpse.

"The neurolizer went off?" he asked, later taking her vivid silence to stand in for another yes.

"It was on full blast. He was gone by the time i got there. Meeko says brain dead," she mentioned. "It's my stupid fault. If i hadn't suggested he make the pulses last a little longer, he would still be here. It's my fault."

"Don't say that."

"Why, because it's true?" she tormented herself. "I was the one. I suggested he make the pulse last because they disappeared too quickly even when I knew there was nothing wrong with his invention like Meeko said, but I...I just thought spending time with him in the labs kept him away from Lydia long enough to keep him busy with me," she admitted with a forlorn look, and one of regret, but not hate, "it was our thing. or supposed to be. Now i've taken him away from the both of us."

"Is Lydia your..." Hrth had begun speaking but didn't see the need to finish that question. In fact, he didn't know what to say that would be appropriate to console Pytrice. It just seemed keeping her company was more than enough.

"She pretends to be."

"I see...er..so...er...who are the others?" Hrth asked to change the subject and rescue her from grief. And it was a welcomed respite because Pytrice took it kindly.

"forerunners. Meeko says every one of them has lived here," she answered and Hrth could hear the relief in her thin voice.

"And they are all dead?"

"technically. Meeko says most of them died in times of the plagues."

"What kind of plague?"

"Many kinds i guess," Pytrice answered sombrely. "There are people here i do not know. Never even met, so i don't look. It gives me bad memories when i sleep."

"You mean dreams—bad dreams?" he corrected.

"Whatever."

"I see," he said and they stood there watching or secretly counting the capsules. "You know I'm sorry for your cat, Pytrice? I didn't know," Hrth said a little while after. This time unlike the last, the apology seemed to roll out by itself. He'd meant it and she knew he'd meant it because she let him call her Pytrice without flipping.

"Everybody dies," she answered succinctly, her tone suggestive she'd accepted his remorse. "Even Kyno."

"Everybody dies," Hrth murmured in chant, before letting a big one escape from his lungs, "Meeko says he can get us back home, so you know if we get back home your father technically doesn't have to die. Nobody has to die if we get it right. In fact, this entire place will be empty by the time you're born," Hrth remarked, saying this out of tact and in order to inspire her, but not necessarily disillusioned by Meeko's unshakable promise. "It's why I hope him right and Tee Wyr wrong."

She held his hand for the first time and Hrth could feel his arteries pulse. It was almost unbelievable. Beneath her hard, caked exterior, she was just as soft, warm, and spongy as everybody else inside. He held her tightly.

"ol'pops is never wrong," she said without looking at him. Of course, she won't look at him. He hadn't earned her trust that easily, but holding hands was somewhere to begin. All vices resolved.

"So you don't think it's impossible we return?" Hrth demurred with a confused gaze.

"ol'pops is never wrong," she insisted.

"But that's exactly my point, you know? It goes both ways. How can he not be wrong twice? And what about what Tee Wyr says? Even if he finds a way through, you all die."

"That's not how it works, plus it's better than the alternative."

"what alternative?"

"If you stay, we most definitely will die. He and Lydia

don't say it, but i know it. Tee Wyr knows it too. But if you return, Hrth, there's a high probability we might die but it's not an absolute one that we are going to die. He says what's impossible is you being here."

"I'm trying to understand what you said right about now, though i don't want to admit that it bugs me how you do understand this physics stuff and why you're saying it to me?"

"ol'pops says it all the time. We all tend to get it after a gazillion times of hearing him talk nineteen to the dozen about it. It doesn't take a knucklehead to figure out it's not so complicated, unless you'd rather i spoon-feed it to you," she said smugly, trying not to let off her typical mordacious wit.

"I see," he said to her with much disbelief, before tossing out the challenge, "explain it to me."

"Very well," she snorted, taking up the gauntlet, much in an attempt to blow her trumpet in the frozen witness of her deceased father. "it's ol'pops theorem of Scale Mechanics. It simply says every—what's the name of your machine again? the one you came in?"

"Persephone."

"Fine. It means your machine, your Persephone, cannot go back in time before it was made because it didn't exist! That would make things too awkward, so boom! —not ever! But now, if what you say is true, it's already there and you're already here. Get it now? See. It's simple quantum physics," she said in a light air of supremacy.

"And that's Meeko's theorem of Scale Mechanics?"

"Yes," she cheered, folding her hands to a job well done.

"That's all? Nothing more?"

"I just explained it to you. What else is there?" she retorted.

"Okay," Hrth concurred patronizingly, "I can try to understand why we might die if this experiment goes haywire but I don't see the harm to you here. Why is it you have to die if we leave?" he asked pointedly and she stuttered, but then threw her hand gloves at him as he laughed revealing most to all of her poor dentition. "I might be better off asking the autistic kid this question, 'cause the way i see it you're just in the dark as I am," he chided her and she pouted in a bid to keep from smiling, before returning her attention to her father's corpse.

"You should bury him you know," he suggested a little while later in the renewed solemnity.

"What's that?"

"I see, you don't know. We put dead people in the ground. It's a tradition back in our world."

"Green earth?"

"Yes green earth," he consented to her reasoning, "it's what every one of us does when we lose someone. It gives us closure and helps seal the wound, in here," Hrth pointed to his heart, "we do it so that we can carry on with our lives without breaking the bond," he said and immediately he said that, despite the fact she didn't look at him, he could see her curiosity burn like a new star.

"Did you bury your father then?" she asked softly after.

"Yes."

"Did it give you closure?"

"Yes."

"Is it why didn't you cry?" she asked pointedly, but now it was Hrth's turn to stutter in a bout with reasoning. So, just as quickly her curiosity vanished, much in the same way it had sprung up.

"This is how we keep our dead," Pytrice affirmed. "We keep them in cryo."

"I see. Actually, we have mortuaries too, places we freeze our dead. still we bury them. I don't get this though."

"There are many things you don't get," she retorted, sounding terse because he probably couldn't answer her last question.

"sorry, my mistake." Hrth chose to apologize.

"Ol' pops says we've been preserving our forerunners in advent we stumble upon the technology to revive and repair whatever sustains their animation."

"like a cryobank? That's a big wish."

"It's tradition. And it's ol'pops' not mine," she replied when Meeko and Lydia popped behind the glass window, staring into the chamber to see if they were in there. Meeko had come to remind Hrth of their little task and Hrth nodded. In fact, he'd completely forgotten about that and so took Pytrice by the hand.

"We need to go," he says.

escape velocity

Hrth was beginning to grow something in the similitude of a beard. "I thought we fixed these shutters months ago?" he asked her as the brightly burning suns beamed down gloriously over sand land. There was no wind today and for miles and miles as far as the eyes can see, all lay barren. Not a gust of wind or flick of sand in the air. They exchanged apparatus as they hung from the shutters, a great many feet above the ground, and Pytrice put the sealing equipment against the glass dome sealing each new chink in the structure within her reach. They had been taking directions from Tee Wyr who on the other hand was inside the glass dome, facing up and directing the climbers to where each chink was.

"That's what happens when you have crawlers around," she answered as she poured another filling of sand into the equipment and waited for the equipment to heat up the silicon until a clear vicious liquid followed through. Pytrice then used the liquid to blend even wherever there was a chink across the surface of the glass. "There have been a lot of them lately," she admitted and reached to finger off some sand Hrth had on his face, before handing him the equipment to help seal the chinks her shorter arms couldn't reach. In turn, he handed her the plasma neurolizer which she secured beneath her armpit.

"I see. Why do you think they come?" he asked and she

shrugged.

"They're stupid scavengers, what else? They don't need any stupid reason to move around."

"How do you propose they climbed this thing then? It's too smooth and curved," Hrth mentioned as he sealed yet another chink and she lifted her palms to him.

"They have these palms," she said before pointing at his boots, "with suckers on them like those boots you're wearing."

"Suckers?"

"Hmm. They can climb anything," she commented, but then rapping at the glass and angrily at Tee Wyr who'd abandoned his duty from below to go the control port and place a video mail to ol'pops and Haku. It appeared ol'pops saw her calling for Tee Wyr's attention from way up the glass structure because Tee Wyr soon turned around, pointed the duo to were the next chink was then gesticulated she allow him an extra minute.

It was the easier and less precarious option for the techie to spot the chinks from within the confines and comfort of the dome, but it was hot outside—so hot, she refused his request, "no minute! no! no! no! stop talking to the knucklehead," she protested, though he couldn't hear her from way down there, and behind such hard thick glass.

"Calm down, Pytrice. Hope you haven't forgotten we're still on this thing," Hrth mentioned, restraining her hand from hitting the glass any further.

"Hah! I just want to kill him sometimes!" she retorted, handing Hrth the gun as he handed her the sealing device, and they both carefully unlocked a boot to proceed a step further over the glass and then locked that very boot before safely unlocking the other in suite. These special gravity boots were how they manuevered the glass dome.

"You know he likes you."

"Who?" she retorted like she knew nothing of whom to which he inferred, yet betrayed by the frown she put on as if she'd intended to spit his face for what he was about say.

Hrth knocked his head for her to look down the glass and unmistakably she looked straight at the video mail with Haku speaking behind the screen. "Him?" she hissed, hiding a blush and getting busy with the sealing device. "I don't like the knucklehead. He smells of welt wheat," she lied.

He laughed but when she tried grabbing the neurolizer, he swung it away from her grip. "Too slow. Not this time, you threaten me you won't," he teased, and so she threatened him with the hot sealing thingy instead. "Careful Pytrice! You want us to fall?"

"It's your fault for saying something that crazy," she shot at him with a misshapen grin.

"You know all this fuss you're making is telling me what i want to know?" he teased again.

"You're lying," she demurred and went back to the

business of sealing chinks in the glass.

"It's just the same way he throws a fuss over any silly little thing i do anytime you're around, am i lying? To know it took me a month to figure that out, that's just depressing," he said to her, ever keeping his distance since she eyed the neurolizer.

Hrth couldn't stop grinning and in her own special way neither could she, but Horus was burning hot enough to build a sweat. Really hot. "There's going to be a cMe today," she surmised, the little blonde intent on changing the subject.

"You know each time you've said that, you've always turned out wrong. if Myk had said that, i would have believed him."

"Maybe you should take the knucklehead and not me the next time Meeko asks you to fix the roof, since he's so brilliant."

"I doubt that."

****

"You need to remember it's primarily a displacement machine. It wasn't intended to leap time but to bridge space. So let's try it again, Haku," Meeko said, the scientist looking on keenly with mechanical eyes that did just a little more than peer at him.

"v plus nine pi against the cube root of nr plus one plus the—"

"When you say nr plus one are you referring to a parenthesis or no parenthesis?" he quizzed.

"er—yes, in parenthesis. They're together."

"Right, but that's why you have to be really clear when letting them know this equation. You can't channel energy if they miss it. One false impression and the machine wouldn't work. Horus forbid it goes fission."

"Okay. I'll get it right, Dr. Meeko. All i need is time."

"You'll have it, but just get it right."

"Okay, can I try again?"

"Of course. Go."

"v plus 9 pi against the cube root of nr plus one— parenthesis—plus the integral total of 64 of v to the power 14 minus 24 of v cube against the minor parenthesis of two r minus one all under the integral total of the root double of r against c," he read off memory without having to look at the holographed equation.

"Right. Nice twist at the end how you were able to break up the integral not to lose the integrity of the equation, but that's good."

"It's how you taught me to do it."

"True," Meeko grinned and rapped against his thigh, "Okay now we move on to parameters—1, 2, 3, go—?"

"where nr plus one—parenthesis—is a complex number and r, c, and v are constants," Haku said with a thrilling smile and Meeko beamed at Haku, his irises in jumbo size through those mechanical lens.

"What constants are r, c and v?"

"r is the radius of the earth. C is speed of light and v is escape velocity!" he buzzed like a bee.

"Right, my boy! You've just about saved us," he said and Meeko attempted to lift Haku off his feet in amazement. His old bones couldn't but they laughed anyway. "Moving on," he flicked a button and the complex equation gave way to a 3D hologram of the Milky Way, "now where should they look? Here?"

"no, that's the Milky Way," Haku replied sternly.

He toggled view to the next ecliptic galaxy.

"Good...you need to let them know to look directly to our neighbouring galaxy for the Hermatic star system," he said before asserting himself strongly, "Here is where you need to let them look. There's no more suited planet or moons for life and our survival than the ones they'll find at the Hermatic Star system, so don't let them waste any more time looking elsewhere. We've spent centuries doing that. They'll just have to take your word for it."

"eh..Dr. Meeko. There's kind of something I've always had in mind to tell you just in case you succeed in getting us back."

"Tell me. What is on your mind?"

"My country is usually condemned for fraud by the many other countries we know back home. They won't even give us a chance to speak for ourselves or speak in our defence, so I'm not sure if anyone will listen to me or my brother because of that."

Meeko grabbed Haku by the shoulder and said, "rubbish! You my boy are an impressive young man. You're the most lovable person I've ever met. They would be crazy not to see that. Besides, you're a citizen of the world and have Persephone. They will be lucky to have you to guide them."

Ruke smiled. "Dr, Meeko, I think I'm the only person you've ever met," he added wittily.

"and yes you are," the scientist beamed back. "Ok. Now we move to referencing..." he said but one of the display screens in unit 15 flicked on so he pushed the real time mail button. Tee Wyr came up flashing a smile and proper dentition on the display screen, though Ruke could see Pytrice way across the background, trying to fix the dome at the same time looking to draw some kind of attention to herself. She was with Hrth. "What's on your mind?" Meeko asked the techie.

"It's Lydia."

"I think she needs him to turn around," Haku interrupted and Meeko advised Tee Wyr take a look at his repair team.

"Oh, I'll get back to them Meeko. I just wanted to let you know Lydia's on her way to unit 15. Myk's had another fit but she says something's up. She's on the hoverbot right now. She summoned it so don't bother looking. Thought I'd give you a heads up," he informed, winking at Haku and Haku winked back, before harrumphing. "She's not in the best of moods today."

"Point taken," Meeko said and turned to the little winker,

"now back to referencing..." he said.

****

The next video mail to come through was marked personal and too many display screens away for comfort. "What's between the two of you nowadays?" Meeko asked and his question caused Haku to grin behind a hidden smirk, as the early teen left to go insert his thumbprint to take the more private video call from Tee Wyr. "Be back in a minute," Meeko counselled when Lydia stepped off the hoverbot with sickened Myk in the lead who was mute as a donkey.

"Hello," Haku said as he waltzed by but hadn't noticed whether Lydia returned his greeting.

"You have the shots?" she requested even before getting to Meeko and the scientist slapped what functioned similarly to a cabinet, to pull out an injection gun. He handed it her.

"How's he?" he asked concernedly, but she injected Myk with five shots of medication and sat him down first before answering.

"I haven't figured out what it is yet but he's limp, he's not said a word all day, and now he's running a fever."

"You think it's the soup? Tee Wyr mentioned last night's soup tasted funny."

"I don't know, but it better not be," she threatened.

"You don't have to be belligerent, Lydia."

"The last time i checked we're not a growing number. These are not times for Pytrice's slipups, Meeko."

"I'll have her take a look at the greenhouse to see if everything's okay the moment she's returns from the dome, but you might have forgotten Tee Wyr mentioned Haku and Hrth having a scuffle there once. They might have knocked things around, still we'll need to give them some rope—now that you mentioned it those two should be back by now," Meeko mentioned, looking for the QC75 in the cabinet and handing it to her to help plug up the needle wound when the hatch sealed itself shut and four asynchronous steps came down the ladder. "Right. They are here."

"We sealed it good as new, but we are having too much damage to that old thing. Anyhow if the shutters don't work properly anymore, that's it ol'pops," Pytrice informed as she returned the neurolizer right to storage without noticing Myk on a bench. "There's nothing more we can do about that. Tell 'em Hrth."

"Whoa! What's up with Myk?" Hrth asked on spotting Myk sitting with a quick dry patch across his forearm and Lydia tried to smile for him.

"Come help me with him," Meeko answered instead. "I suspect it's a mild case of food poisoning, but we're still trying to figure that out."

"food poisoning? Doesn't that mean we might be sick too?"

"I wouldn't expect that. We all didn't have the same dinner last night," Meeko remarked before requesting Pytrice to go to the greenhouse.

The funny thing was Hrth had actually offered to do so

when Pytrice simpered, "I don't know what you guys think is wrong with the knucklehead, but I haven't even taken off my boots yet." Only for Lydia to rise and land one smack across Pytrice's left cheek, without actually intending to.

"I said stop calling him that!" she said abruptly before realizing the disturbing trigger she just pulled. It had been an off the cuff reaction to an off the cuff remark, so immediately Lydia reached to apologize but Pytrice escaped her touch.

"I hate you! You're not my mother, Lydia! and not my stepmother! You will never be! I hate you! I just hate you!" she bellowed, reacting strongly and tears pooling in her eyes, even as she stormed off to the terminal gateway; most probably on her way to the greenhouse. So within the steady lingering of the eyes Hrth assisted Meeko in laying Myk on his back.

"What's up with those two?" he asked, looking for conservation to bridge the spine-chilling lull building amidst them since Haku on the other hand was in an engaging conversation with Tee Wyr not too far a distance away.

"I asked the same thing myself," Meeko said and went to break up the covert conversation. Unfortunately, Haku and Tee Wyr had been so locked in conversation they couldn't have seen the scientist coming. Or hit the escape key in time.

‾boiling point‾

"You remember this?" Tee Wyr asked, forwarding his symphony of frequencies to Haku's display.

"of course."

"Do you see it?"

"I see it now."

"Are you sure? Take a closer look," he said, a look of anxiety about face.

"It looks the same to me, Tee Wyr. I don't see anything," Haku answered taking a much closer look at the sinusoidal flips and amplitudes on the screen.

"Look again. It's almost the same, except for the 6 second hiatus i inserted to separate the pulses. Don't you remember?"

"Oh yea, i remember that. Okay, I'm looking at it now— whoa, that's new i think. What's that?"

"Exactly. Now, you see it too. I got those this morning," Tee Wyr said anxiously.

"I don't understand. I thought it was your signal?"

"it is. it's just that now i see these other signals when I'm not transmitting."

"What do you mean when you're not transmitting? You're always transmitting, aren't you?"

"Yes, but I transmit in cycles so those minor waves are not supposed to be in my 6 second window. You're the only one I've shown this to. What do you think?"

"eh, i don't know. What do you think?" Ruke asked back.

"I think it's them," Tee Wyr stated anxiously.

"What do you mean them?—crawlers?"

"Yea. I mean it's them i wrote it for, right?"

"So what you think is they are like speaking? I see your point."

Tee Wyr drew in a deep breath. "I want to show you something," he said and cut off his feed, but after he'd done that the minor waves mulishly remained. "You see?"

"Whoa! It's still there."

"We're supposed to be the only ones out here, Haku."

"You killed the feed?"

"Yes."

"Whoa buzzkill."

"That's all i thought all morning."

"okay, so we assume they are the ones speaking, but who are they're speaking to then? I thought they weren't so intelligent?"

"You know I've always guessed they were, right? but not like this."

"I don't like these funny vibes."

"You're not the only one."

"You are the one who started the signals, do you think

they might be trying to communicate with you and not themselves?" Haku asked and a visible sweat zigzagged its way down Tee Wyr's face.

"No way, but I thought about that too," he replied tensely. "It's could be either, but whichever way makes me wonder how many of them are really out there? That's what gets me, Haku. We seldom have one or two crawlers snooping about a month, but this."

"I know. What worries me is if they are as intelligent like you say they are, and can hear your signals as clearly as music like you said they do, what's to stop them from coming here looking for it?" Haku mentioned and Tee Wyr exhaled deeply.

"Ouww...I never saw it that way. I just may have put us in a lot of trouble."

"Do you think we should tell Dr. Meeko?" Haku suggested.

"I don't think that will be a good idea. Let's wait it out, first. Meeko's very gentle but even he has a boiling point. I don't think he'll forgive me if he knew," Tee Wyr admitted when all of a sudden his entire face flushed red in colour.

"You don't have to tell me anything," Meeko said when he came up from behind Haku with the impression of a scowl across his face. Haku stuttered but Meeko dismissed the early teen to the greenhouse before throwing the burden of his frown at Tee Wyr. "I want to see you here and now," he revealed silently, speaking not with his lips but with his fingers, boiling even hotter when he let the words slip from his mouth.

****

"You know she didn't mean that?"

Lydia tried to smile as she sat by Myk, holding his warm hand, "I know Hrth."

"With the way she talks about you, i think it's because you remind her of her dad."

"She talks about me?"

"Yes. More than she's willing to admit," he said and for the first time today Lydia showed the promise of a smile. "It's why i think she takes it so hard whenever you're disappointed at her. She has a very low breaking point."

"Oh Hrth, I love her each day as much as i loved her father. I'm not disappointed at her. I would never."

"She thinks so."

"oh no," she uttered,"...then it's my fault."

"eh..i think so too," Hrth concurred for a crack at humour and it worked. It did elevate her gloom. "No. There are some things about Pytrice we are never going to be able to change. She survives by not showing a shred of emotion. I figured that out months ago."

"In many ways, i think the two of you are alike," Lydia mentioned after a little silence.

"You think?"

"You both don't always have to hang out together for anyone to figure that out."

"I see."

"I hope you realize that when you leave it's going to have a big effect on her? You're the only person she's bonded to she rarely picks a fight with."

"I noticed that. May be it's because i've figured out her weak spots," Hrth said, gesticulating by boxing the air. "I think she's lovely."

"then you should have met David. He was just like her. Even worse. Uncouth aside being stubborn. He made you love him though. He had this way of winning your heart," Lydia snapped her fingers, "just like that."

"What happened to her mother? I've never been able to ask her that."

"Wise you didn't. Pytrice never got to meet her mother. She died before Pytrice was born. I raised her."

"I see."

"Her name was Dylyan. She was more of an architect than anything else. You must have figured we're jacks of all trade here, we learn what we can from who we can, but she had this special gift to build things and loved to draw arcs and sketches."

"What killed her?"

"Crawler fever."

"oh."

"Pytrice was just 5 months when it happened. I tried to save her. Meeko did too, but she was just too far gone. She'd not only been cut, she'd been eaten into. The infections were impossible to stop."

"So how did you end up saving Pytrice?"

"Cross-section surgery. After David and I removed the foetus we placed it in one of our live incubators at cryo."

"You grew her?" Hrth asked, astonished.

"Yes, if you say it like that, but we can also do that with any fertilized cell."

"We call it a test tube baby back at home, it's a miracle you guys can do that so easily now. It's sketchy science. Is that kind of what you did for him? I've never heard you talk about his father?" Hrth asked but Lydia kind of shrugged off the question so he let it slide, yet his words seemed to jolt Myk from his temporary platitude.

"Sketchy science. Test tube baby!" Myk parroted but from the expression on Lydia's face, his little outburst was priceless. In fact, Lydia broke a tear.

****

She snarled when the blast doors slid open and Haku bounced right into the UV lit greenhouse. "What are you doing here?" a voice boomed from the shadows.

"Dr. Meeko sent me."

"Well go back, knucklehead. You can see I'm already here," she stated, requesting her time alone in as much as demanding for it.

"Why is it you have to be so hostile every time?" Ruke retorted offhandedly, redirecting his attention to the special bouquets trapped behind glass cylinders and fed constantly with distilled water.

"Because you don't listen," she grunted, watching the intransigent knucklehead go ahead to inspect the bouquets. "I said go back!"

"You don't have to like me, I get it," he responded artlessly, "but I'm not Hrth. I'm not going anywhere because you feel like it. And I don't know why you always have to be so cold to everyone all the time. It's crazy!"

She watched him move between the seedlings with a grim stare, her hands clenched into a fist, sourly missing her neurolizer, yet he moved on listlessly, enervated by her threats.

"I'd like to say I get you, but i don't. You're not the only one here. We've all lost one parent or another, so that's no excuse from what i think," he said and again artlessly. He couldn't see her within the shadows of the UV lit greenhouse, but surely felt her gaze dog his every step wherever she may be. It unnerved him. She was Pytrice, not too far from belligerent and predictably so. "Where are you?" he demanded now taking every moment to swing a glance in any and every direction. Just in case.

"You don't know anything about me," Pytrice snarled.

"Okay. Maybe i don't know, but pushing everyone who's trying to help you anyway isn't helping," he said when Haku thought he spotted a shadow whisk behind him. "Will you come out and stop this?" he demanded nervously.

"Stop what," she rejoined.

"Stop this. This game you're playing. Show yourself. Where are you?"

"I warned you."

"This! This is what I'm talking about. This is why you're so weird! This is why no one likes you!"

"No one likes me?" she intonated with a ring.

"Yes," Haku swallowed down hard before bravely repeating himself, "yes. No one likes you."

"That's not what your brother says," she intonated again and snickered.

"What do you mean not what my brother says?"

"You don't know?" she teased, dancing somewhere in the shadows.

"Know what?"

"He says you like me—like really really like me, that's why you act all goofy," she taunted him.

"That's a lie," Haku shot back impulsively, almost in defence of his honour, but why he'd done so, and yet again so aggressively, he couldn't explain.

"I'm ready if you want to kiss me," she tormented him, smacking and puckering her lips from the sound of her.

Haku grew livid even as he flushed with embarrassment. "You're impossible!" he shot at her wanting to get out of the greenhouse before his tear ducts gave out.

But as if her taunting wasn't enough, she threw a ball of

something at him when he opened the blast doors with his fingerprints to leave. It hit him at the base of the neck and she came out of the darkness just enough for him to see her smiling devilishly at him. "I thought you wanted to stay?" she snickered with an air of victory on winning this standoff.

"you don't scare me," he said to her bravely but instantly couldn't take back his choice of words.

"I don't have to," she smiled broadly and like an epiphany Ruke could see it in her eyes. In a strange way, he'd lifted her spirits and that unnerved him a lot on realizing the little red-haired blonde under the Near Red lights fed on weakness. He'd only now shown her his, although his brother was just as much to blame for this. So he stood there trembling and glowering at her even to boiling point as she glowered back at him like a mirror; all emotions reciprocated.

signals

The scientist was almost trembling as he paced about and pacing terribly. It sufficed in keeping Tee Wyr rooted to his seat somewhere between both adults, taking the scolding with a fallen face. Hrth hadn't seen the bleach-haired old man more flushed.

"How could you even think such a thing? You've endangered all our lives—and our lives are not as important endangering their lives! You've short-changed our future!"

Tee Wyr ventured to speak but Meeko cut him off, still pacing, and pacing terribly, "no! No excuses!"

"You have to believe, i didn't intend it. I've been shooting these signals a long time before they arrived—"

"I said no excuses!" the scientist interpolated and turned to Lydia who equally looked disappointed, but not disappointed enough for Meeko. "Don't you have anything to say?"

Lydia wasn't smiling yet she had a much lighter mood about her, probably because her son was perched atop her thighs eating welt wheat. "You of all people should know what you've done is pretty serious, Tee Wyr," she said, trying to squeeze in a frown somewhere.

"I know but would you even listen to me? I'm sorry—I honestly wouldn't put Haku and Hrth in danger, Meeko. Please. You have to believe me."

"What i believe is what i see. And what i see is you

drawing attention to us. You pray to Horus they don't come this way—you pray you haven't jeopardize all what we've put together these three months," Meeko shot at him when Haku returned from the greenhouse.

"But he said he was sorry, Dr. Meeko," the early teen butt in straight away, yet with the expression Hrth could garner from the moulage off the face of a maddened scientist, he grabbed Haku by the arm and took him away for a more private talk between brothers. Meeko turned to Tee Wyr, "have you stopped the broadcasting?" he demanded.

"Yes. Of course. I did so immediately I got the back feed."

"Did you record any of it?"

"Yes, i did," Tee Wyr was forced to admit, and ruefully.

"Show me. I want to see it," he requested, but Tee Wyr was already on it before the scientist had finished talking and Lydia threw Meeko the old forgiving face. Maybe there was redemption after all, despite the fact Tee Wyr had not only encrypted the audio files but buried them somewhere both she and Meeko would have never guessed the next gazillion years. The recorded signals popped up via the hologram screen, and as Meeko turned and tuned the waves as he saw fit, his little secret was out.

****

Haku wriggled himself off Hrth's grip immediately the brothers were out of earshot and back at the INS

Control Centre, having haggled over what was moral and what could have been the proper course of action. "It is still quite serious for Lydia and Meeko to be upset like that. You're equally culpable in this because you kept this strictly between you two. What if something had gone wrong?"

"Okay, but nothing went wrong. I don't see why Dr. Meeko's so livid. We all makes mistakes, don't we?"

"Everyone's allowed a couple of mistakes, yes, but not foolish ones. Don't you want to go home?" Hrth asked and for some reason the question seemed to prick his younger brother like a needle as Haku's dark and caramel face shrunk into a tight ball.

"Don't even ask me that."

"You see? This isn't just about getting home. It is way beyond us now and what we want. Look at me and tell me if you honestly think Meeko would forgive himself if anything happened to us? This is the fate of the world we're talking about, Ruky. Our petty secrets don't matter."

"Okay, but what do you mean our secrets don't matter?"

"cause they don't. I don't get you."

"Why would you tell that misanthrope that i like her or something like that?"

"misanthrope?"

"Yes."

"because it's true. And she's not a misanthrope, Ruky,

Besides, that's nothing to be embarrassed about."

"No, that's a lie," Haku retorted angrily, trying not to look into those glassy eyes when strong-arming his brother into an apology.

"then i was wrong. I'm sorry?"

"You should know what she's like when you tell her things like that. You shouldn't be talking to her about me," he fumed, so Hrth deciding to take the gentle approach took his brother by the hands.

"you know you're not the only one with secrets if that's the case. She's a test tube baby!" Hrth said and Haku's jaw almost fell off.

"Oh my god!" Haku mouthed after the gape.

"You know she'd kill you if she knew you knew that? And me for telling you that, right?"

Haku pressed a finger against his lips and shook his head in promise not to utter a single word of it, and both brothers shared knuckles. Almost the same giggle.

"I want us to get home. They need us to get home, so we have to be careful here. We need to let them help us," Hrth said softly and in kind of an apologetic tone.

"I know," Haku had to agree, both brothers still holding hands. "I think i should apologize for my part in this."

"I think Meeko would like that very much," Hrth said, almost swallowing up his brother in an embrace.

"You think i should go now?"

"Eh...I don't think now would be a good time. They are

still—you know," he shrugged and leaned against the wall, or what they knew to be the munitions shelf closed up into the wall, when it gave off a very familiar sound. "Whoa!" they both seemed to say as it generously opened up, ejecting its contents to fulfil a request they'd apparently made.

"You got the passcode. How did you do that?" Haku asked excitedly almost too eager to rub this into Pytrice's face.

"I don't know. I don't think she intended it to be a difficult passcode. 'must have depressed the right buttons when i leaned into this thing," Hrth confessed and looked at what was now a table of equipment. "These ones look odd. They are not cells for neurolizers that's for sure."

"No. They are projectile rounds," came the ever familiar voice from across the adjoining entrance to Unit 8, flashing a mocking glance at Haku who didn't hesitate to cast bold eyes back at her as well. Somehow she looked stunned he could still look her full in the face.

"you mean bullets? Bullets for guns?" he asked her, quite surprised, as she ambled over to be by his side. As usual, Hrth took her silence to signify an answer, "i thought you said you guys never had those here."

"Ha! You can never believe what she says. You should know that by now," Haku interjected even as she eyed him.

"I said those guns don't work on crawlers, not that we don't have them. These were for the old folk, but my dad changed all that when he figured they were practically useless," she stated matter-of-factly only for Haku to interject her again.

"then why haven't you guys thrown them all away, if they had been so useless?"

She attempted to stare him down. "They are too loud. And those crawlers have reinforced carbon for bones and a high tolerance for pain. Ask Lydia and she'll tell you. Those guns don't even slow them down. You best pray you never have to face one, knucklehead," she cautioned, still wondering why Ruke was staring at her awkwardly. She looked to Hrth. "How come you learned it without telling me? Nobody knows that passcode but me."

"Beginner's luck i guess," he answered. "I don't think you made it to be that complicated. Now where are they?—these projectile guns?"

"Second shelf beneath the first, but you need to know the second passcode to bring it out," she apprised, almost eager to see him try.

****

"And you say those minor frequencies were never yours," Meeko said, delacing the frequencies and isolating the wavelengths by their amplitudes.

"Yes," Tee Wyr answered obsequiously and almost swore it so.

"There's nothing else?"

"No."

"Do you still have your receiver tuned?"

"It always live."

"Fine. Let it run. I want to see it," Meeko said and immediately the readings that popped up startled them.

"That wasn't there before," Tee Wyr was forced to confess. His dimunitive 6-second readings of sinusoidal feedbacks were now a live cycle of undulating amplitudes and regular frequencies. Whatever he'd attempted to do when he stopped airing his frequencies, looked abortive. On the other hand, whatever seemed to generate these new frequencies sought to re-establish some sort of connection with his melodies.

"Lydia," Meeko called. "What do you make of this? They look like multiple frequencies but when i isolate the frequencies, they all have their individual timeframes. Look."

Lydia let Myk eat by himself and moved to study the leftover frequencies, "it can't be. It appears they are communicating with one another."

"Not very far from my hypothesis. Each frequency's sustained. Sustained communication is a demonstration of intelligence, don't you think?"

"I don't know, but if they can do this anything's possible," she admitted, a growing consternation abroad her face.

"I'm beginning to doubt those incidents at the other facilities. It's my guess that incident at the remote islands was anything but accidental," Meeko stated and Tee

Wyr took a deep breath. "Then again, it's possible we use this mishap to our advantage."

"What do we do?" Tee Wyr asked, quick and servile.

"Can you piggyback on the frequency?" Meeko asked when the PA system chimed: New Alert; proximate search complete; one displacement module found; 5° 30' N; 5°45 E; five thousand pascals; recalibrating model distance; 3 ten to the power 6 light-years away; model name: Persephone; now initializing protocol.

Meeko couldn't jump for joy at the news like Lydia could, but he went ahead to hug Tee Wyr, and the young man shed a tear for it. It was done. All the waiting had paid off.

****

When the broadcast ran through the PA system, it ran through the entire facility at about the same time, according to how Meeko had programmed it.

"Did you hear that?"

"Is that what i think it is?" Haku asked. A bewildered look on his face.

"He found it."

"We're going home?"

"Yes. Yes! We're going home!" Hrth concurred and Pytrice watched the brothers hug, jump, and dance. They looked so excited and had been so happy, they hardly took notice of the little blonde when she slipped out the exit; leaving them more room to air box and do all the crazy stuff boys do.

chaos theory

A multicolour of hypodermic syringes lay in wait beside the injection gun in the infirmary and in the neat row she had arranged them, Lydia was set to run through every one of them. The previous shot was just the third of the set, so Hrth stretched forth his hand again and the molecular biologist meticulously sterilized another patch of Hrth's chocolaty skin. Lydia picked up the gun, replaced the empty syringe with a purple one and shot the bubbly bio-fluid into his bloodstream.

"Is this medical check really necessary? You make it seem like my brother and I are travelling to space or something like that?" he asked and Lydia revealed quite a generous amount of teeth while pumping the fourth syringe into his forearm.

"We can't be too careful, Hrth. This is all a precautionary procedure. It might not have mattered when you came here, but we can't have you going back with some kind of infection or virus from this place. This IV in particular is to sterilize you from such hostile infections, if in case you carry some in your bloodstream," she replied as she engaged the next watery load. This one looked viscous and was surprising painful when she shot it through the veins feeding his fingers on the backside of his palm.

Hrth flinched, but he didn't say. He just braced himself for the next shot. "You mean future viruses?"

"Yes. Our eras are different. There's no use sending you two back in time only to have you kick-start some kind of global pandemic. It defeats the whole purpose of your coming here, if you get my point."

"I see."

He flinched again after she emptied the pellucid yellow syringe, so she sort of winked at him when reaching for the milky one.

"You're not one to complain, are you Hrth? We are all on our feet on this one since Rostov was able to get you here. Meeko wants to be sure we secure ourselves against damaging off-shoots of the chaos theory, so you'll have to bear with me a little while longer. This will all be over in a few seconds," she remarked and immediately the late teen shook the disconcertment off his face.

"It's nothing, Lydia. Don't worry about me complaining."

"That's the spirit," she muttered, swapping one arm for the other.

"Sounds dangerous, the way you say it—this chaos theory. What is it?" he asked when she picked up the sixth syringe and tapped the vial to secure its bubbles, if there be any, to one end.

"I think you'll be better off asking Meeko that," she confessed to him, before requesting Hrth clench then release his fist, which he did, enabling Lydia to jab the purple syringe up a new vein. "Do you feel dizzy?" she asked.

"No. Should I?"

"You will in a couple of minutes, so sit properly," she

advised, so Hrth straightened up in what could suffice as both a recliner and stretch bed. He looked around the infirmary. It was as a typical clinic back at home with containers and apparatus he could make little sense of. They were all neatly arranged in their varied places of use, and alphabetically labelled from A to P. The labelling ended abruptly at P.

"Have you seen Pytrice, doctor?" Hrth asked and Lydia nodded.

"I saw her yesterday. Why do you ask?"

"It might sound awkward but I haven't seen her lately. Then again neither have i seen Tee Wyr. I suppose everyone's been busy with our return," he mentioned.

"that's the Pytrice we know, though Meeko's had her and Myk help with the recalibrations of the fission cells down at the reactor rooms that work the time-displacement machines for your journey back. So if you're looking for her, you'll probably find her there," she answered, taking up a red hypodermic syringe before swabbing another patch of skin.

"I see."

"But if she's avoiding you, Hrth, I suspect she must have a reason to," Lydia muttered.

"I actually haven't given it a second thought, but this place is not really that big. To think of it, I think she's avoiding me."

"You think?" Lydia chimed back and her choice of words sounded vaguely familiar.

"I see. I get it now."

Lydia cocked her head at him. "You should. Unless you want to tell me you've forgotten our last conversation so soon?" she said as she injected the painless shot into his right shoulder and the vivacity faded from his face, "don't let the blood drain from your face, Hrth. You haven't left yet. You still have a couple of days."

"Actually i don't know what to say to her," Hrth confessed as Lydia reached for the seventh and last syringe.

"Goodbyes are never easy," Lydia said, pumping him full of the pink fluid inside it, and in effect the room began to spin, as if on an axis, when he attempted reaching for the door. Luckily, she was there to keep him from falling, but all Tagho could think about was getting to the little blonde.

****

As he'd come to expect, Meeko and Haku were at the INS Control Centre revising notes as had been the usual routine for the last number of days. Hrth hadn't wanted to intrude because the scientist never looked more alive and pretty much beamed with life; a feeling that went both ways for Hrth could argue his brother's glowing face was just itching to put a smile on Meeko's face. The pair went together like akpu and egusi, and he stood a good distance away contemplating the impact leaving this place might have on that bond. Or the brother he knew, so to speak.

"Rostov's a genius. If only we had more of his brain. The

computer's feeding me data right from 1987 your era."

"1987? That's a long time away."

"Right."

"I wasn't even born then?" Haku asked again, confused, and Meeko chuckled.

"I don't think he was expecting you specifically, Haku. He shot it 20 years past your time with hope someone in the least would encounter his machine," he mentioned and something in the early teen's silence spoke infinitely loud. "Tell me. What's on your mind?".

"Dr. Meeko...would it be possible to send us back to before we came?"

"Certainly, that was the agreement I remember. Your request was two weeks before you came, if I'm correct?"

"yes, but that's not what I'm asking about. I have this crazy thought that's kind'f popped into my head. To tell the truth actually, I've got myself thinking about it a while because when i look around all I see is everyone putting their backs to ensuring we get home."

"oh. You want me to send you back to a time before your time?" Meeko inferred with a contorted smile across his face.

"Yes. You said Rostov shot Persephone 20 years before we came, right? Why don't we use that 20 years as...eh...eh..."

"you mean as some kind of failsafe? A kind of error margin for you to get the job done in time?"

"Yes. That's what i mean."

"That's kind of you, Haku, but no. All we require is that you make sure you're heard. Actually, i have no doubt that you will be heard. Don't worry about it. Two weeks is fine."

"But we have this chance?"

"Haku, it's too risky."

"But why? Why not Dr. Meeko?"

"Because that risk is what we know as the chaos theory, Haku. In theory, we'd be pushing our limits," the scientist was forced to admit, to his own chagrin, beginning to see the growing rift that made him less and less of a daredevil Rostov and more and more of the failsafe Meeko. So much so Meeko apologized for it, "i'm sorry."

"I'm sorry too Dr. Meeko. I didn't mean to push. I hadn't thought it was that difficult."

"it's not, Haku. It's not your fault. I just can't take a risk with your safety, that's all. You see the chaos theory is this complex of natural systems that obey rigid rules, and so sensitive that even a small initial change can trigger unexpected final results, thus giving the illusion of randomness as a way to counteract and balance that change."

"Oh."

"Do you know the percentage probability for a germ cell to fertilize one simple human ovum, Haku?"

"I'm guessing 50-50," Haku said, bewildered by the

question, though the scientist looked him in the eye pensively. Almost taking him seriously for a moment.

"You're wrong."

"Truth is I know what an ovum is Dr. Meeko, but what's a germ cell?" he asked and Meeko cocked his head at Haku's crotch.

"euww," Haku muttered, also looking at his crotch.

"it's twenty million to 1. The tendency of every person you know being born is twenty million to one every time we humans try."

"oh."

"What I'm trying to say Haku is the chaos theory works like a bowl of sand. We are that bowl of sand. If you tap it, and one grain of sand pushes the other, you might never get to see your grain of sand ever again. What you see is something else. So in theory, your coming to Sand Land is not near as dangerous as your returning to Green Earth. Rostov bequeathed me with that, but if you return to a time before you were born, that change to the system will trigger an unpredictable response back at green earth. It could be one so dastardly, you may never be born. And if you are not born, Haku, then you will never be here and your novel timeline is lost. It spells disaster for all of us. So we aren't just back to square one, we're worse off. Do you understand what I'm trying to say to you?"

"I think so," Haku lied.

"Don't worry. You will understand when you return

home. As i said, Rostov's a genius. He probably could have found a way to buy you more time, but i have to admit i'm not Rostov. I cannot even dare the game theory because you being here and now is our sure chance for hope! The mechanics of game theory run ad infinitum on so large a scale, I'd have to be half as crazy as Rostov to risk it," he mentioned, again doubting himself.

"You're doing your best, Dr. Meeko," Haku chipped in and Meeko heaved, daring to believe the young teenager. "What's the game theory?"

Meeko chuckled at the young boy's blazing curiosity, "I'll try not to use big words this time. The game theory is like this probability game. It's the probability of having two or more very different outcomes, obviously contradictory outcomes, from opposing variables; much like opposing realities. In your case, to go back in time, even to a time before you were born, doesn't fully conclude you will just disappear. In theory, the game theory assures me you will be both alive and not alive on your return because it's viable for energy to transmute from one form to the other, but i just can't take that risk."

Haku bobbed his head slowly, "err.. how can i be alive and not alive at the same time, Dr. Meeko?"

"Is that too hard as well? i didn't...i didn't simplify it enough, did I?"

"No. I still don't get it," he confessed and Meeko found it amusing.

"It's like i said. Don't worry. You will understand once you've crossed the continuums and returned home. Actually, you'll understand it better than even I, since you'll be the one to experience it firsthand."

"okay, but you know I think you're the best, Dr. Meeko," Haku said in a reinforcement of admiration and to lift the old man's spirits.

"I know," Meeko said and without ado switched sporadically to the mental exercises they had been working through the last couple of days as Haku had come to expect, "do you remember the time-displacement equation?"

"Of course."

"Let me hear it."

"v plus 9 pi against the cube root of nr plus one—nr plus one is in parenthesis—plus the main integral of 64 v to the power 14 minus 24v cube against the minor parenthesis of two r minus one all divided by the root double of r against c, where r, c and v are constants."

"Right," Meeko said, pulling up the 3D hologram of the galaxy in routine.

"Dr. Meeko?"

"What's on your mind?"

"Dr. Meeko, why is it you spend time teaching me all this stuff and not Hrth?" he asked humbly and immediately both brothers shared one heart the moment he said it. And though neither had anticipated an answer, it was odd to notice Meeko couldn't really centre on any answer.

"I think it's because you ask Haku, but why do you ask?"

"It's just that my brother's always away when you're teaching me stuff and I'm beginning to feel like you actually want it that way?" he asked cleverly and the old scientist ran a hand through his bleached hair for once. "I'm not all that—"

"I'm here! I just don't like to intrude when you two are going on with it," Hrth said, deciding now to butt in from behind as something in those words touched him far more than he could ever express. They were still brothers, but not only Meeko could see that in the face of his brother's unhinged idolatrous disposition, Haku had literally reminded the old scientist so.

"Right! See," Meeko tittered.

"Have you seen Pytrice, doctor Meeko? Lydia said she might be at the reactor room, but I'm just coming from the reactor room and she's not there," Hrth mentioned.

"Yes, I had her working on some of the fuel cells. She should still be around someplace," he said switching his 3D galactic hologram for a 3D schematic of the facility in search for the little blonde's last known log.

"I think she's by the hatch. Tee Wyr mentioned something about her going to check the shutters earlier or something like that," Haku mentioned to his brother.

"No. that's surface. Unless she went with Myk? Did she go with Myk?"

"Don't think so."

"that's against the golden rule. No one's supposed to be up there by themselves," Hrth said when Meeko's schematic flashed a crimson red and the computer automatically logged Pytrice out by 2 seconds.

"I think this answers our question," Meeko informed, now attempting to place a video call to the observatory, "but i don't know why she felt she needed to do this alone?" he muttered.

"Let me handle this. I'll get her," Hrth said to the scientist even as he caressed his brother by the nape, "brace up. Doctor Lydia needs you for your shots. She's expecting you at the infirmary."

"I'll be there."

"It's important. She doesn't want you killing all of humanity with diseases you take back with you," he emphasized so Meeko commuted his video call to the infirmary.

"Soon then," Haku promised.

quarantine protocol

The first sign of crawler activity didn't amount to much. It had come as a multiple sequence of numbers that barely made any sense, so whatever depressed those execution codes at the hatch was probably long gone by now. The techie had more urgent things on his mind as he sought to make sense of the impuissant workload streaming through his own terminal, as well as what the scientist required him to do with it. He waited on the data as he would on Meeko—anxious and half confused.

"I actually didn't think she'd go through with it," Tee Wyr explained himself through the display monitor, but ever since the incident Meeko had been clamping down a little too harshly on him.

"She's not where she should be."

"I actually thought the usual. I thought Hrth would be in her company."

"Well he's not."

"Has Hrth gone to get her then?" he asked sheepishly but Meeko expected him to find his own answer, somehow finding it his responsibility for her going awol.

"is it working?" he cut in. "Have you been able to secure the broadcasts yet?"

"No, but that's resolved because i'll have it soon."

"When?"

"A couple of minutes."

"Make sure it's done. These aren't times for slipups," Meeko instructed but that was about the time the communications techie noticed another sequence of random execution codes slipping through the hatch. The punched-in codes seemed to come in circuits, every two or so hours, so Tee Wyr pushed some buttons to investigate. Aside the fact it could have been triggered by almost anything, ranging from a faulty hatch to the cumulative impression of sand across the keys.

The scientist on the other hand was too busy synchronizing the time-displacement machines from his end of the screen to even notice the highlight popping up by the hatch once every two to three hours across his schematic via the hologram table.

"Is she still by the hatch?" Tee Wyr asked curiously.

"No. Pytrice logged out before Haku headed for the infirmary," he mumbled spiritlessly then placing his second video call today to the infirmary just to be certain the early teen was where he should be. It seemed any day could be the day the brothers headed back the way he acted. When he found Haku there, it all fell on his awareness, "Hrth should be back by now. What is it she went up there to do?" Meeko had to ask because the facility being rooted in clandestine origins had no cameras installed above ground.

"she mentioned something about the shutters malfunctioning. Much of the equipment is off, with the bombardment and all. I thought you knew."

"I did, but how come you expect her to do it without assistance?"

"I..I thought Hrth was with her. I thought they had your approval," Tee Wyr beckoned but Meeko didn't smile. Or even seem to agree. He frowned instead.

"That's not what i meant," Meeko said, pointing at the control port behind the techie.

"Oh that. Sorry. I'll get right to it," Tee Wyr confessed ruefully and terminated the video call, and though it was hard to admit, he'd ended the call with quite some relief. Moving on to the sky lens, he opened the shutters to aid Pytrice's repairs from the outside, but the moment the shutters came down, the lenses shattered and they broke in one after the other—crawlers! Four males by the look of it!

They moved too quickly for the techie to think twice.

****

Hrth popped out of the hatch to encounter Pytrice's pretty blond hair caught like static in the wind. It only came to rest by her shoulders after he'd made up the distance between them. The little blonde was building dust devils in the air with Meeko's gravity scooter. They stayed whirring for minutes on end by gravity until a whiff or gust blew them into oblivion.

"These are lovely. What do you call them?"

"Whatever we choose to call them," she muttered, starting over to making new ones in simple routine.

"we call them dust devils back at green earth."

"what do you want Hrth?" she muttered again, already knowing the direction this little banter was headed. The very way she knew in which direction the winds would topple sands.

"I know we're leaving. You don't have to be upset Pytrice."

"You can't tell me what to be Hrth, and i'm not upset," she smacked, as the winds toppled her sands prematurely.

"I see. So you're not even a bit upset?" he inquired and she shook her head vigorously almost as if doing so would make it true. "You're sure about that?" he inquired again, this time reaching to touch her dust devils, but as he'd expected she slapped his arm off.

"Don't touch it," she grunted.

There it was and Hrth could only smile at her. "I see."

"No. You don't see anything, do you?"

"All i see is you're upset."

"And all i see is a fool. I said I'm not upset!" she barked, and so viciously, she destroyed the very dust devil she was trying to create.

"Why am I a fool, Pytrice? Why would you even call me that?"

"You're a fool because you're not coming back! If ol'pops is wrong and that thing doesn't work, you're not coming back!" she snapped lividly.

"But Meeko is never wrong, you said that," Hrth

responded and for a while she had no answer. Not until the little blonde realized she needed not an answer to speak how she felt.

"You're wrong about that."

"I—I'm wrong? Or you're wrong?"

"You should stay here. It's not safe," she grunted, but it was the way she said it that made Hrth think. It seemed she was appealing to him, trying to get him to grow cold feet.

"We're not safe here either. You said that too, more or less."

"What do you want from me Hrth? I'm not going to give you an apology!" she yelled at him, her voice so loud it clawed at his ears.

"I don't want an apology! I just want you to say it."

"Say what?"

"Say you'll miss us after we're gone. That's what's eating into you, isn't it? Admit you'll miss me."

"Don't count on it," she snapped at him again with tears forming at the edge of her eyes. "I'm not going to cry after you when you're gone."

Hrth grabbed Pytrice by the hands forcefully, forcing her to look deeply into those two expressionless black irises, hard as glass and glazed over, "admit you'll miss me, Pytrice. Admit there are some things in life you can never change. Admit it!" he demanded and for the first time a tear slid down those expressionless eyes. She'd never seen Hrth cry before. Not ever.

She did admit something. "Everyone cries," she said as she tore her hands off his grip, but it seemed Hrth hadn't noticed the warm liquid when it streaked down a corner of his eye. He lifted his fingers to it to make certain he was crying, and had this weird smile smack between his lips when he found it so. To him, it was funny. "What? What's funny?"

"This is it."

"this is what?"

"Closure," he admitted and she was quiet. He laughed or cried, she couldn't tell, but watched amazingly as more streaks fell down that one eye. In the strangest of ways, Hrth tears flooded her with the bucolic idyll of what was once a great civilization. Why it caught her totally off guard, she never could tell. Only it never prepared her for what was coming. She totally hugged him!

"Thank you for coming," she cried softly. "I'll miss you," she admitted and there was nothing much to say after that, save for the storm brewing far north and headed their way.

The hatch was malfunctioning. It's touchpad had locked them out, keeping them waiting more than they realized under the suns and in the open hands of Sand Land, which turned out to be the second sign of crawler activity today—but how were they to know that?

****

The power to the observatory went out, that was all Meeko knew, or rather all he saw, because its video feed it went out. He slapped the display monitor just be sure.

"Tee Wyr?" he spoke into the comm. link, only to realize the telecom to the observatory was also out, so the old scientist tried establishing a control connection to other sections of the facility. The connection to the greenhouse went through accordingly; even Myk was at the end of the communicator at the reactor rooms. Talking to Myk was like communicating with a computer, he always needed an execution protocol, "Myk, i'm sending you a bot. Lydia and Haku will be on it. You need to be on it," he instructed, but had barely even finished talking when Myk bounced off the comm. link on the slightest bearing of a pause. He was headed in a beeline for the nearest landing pad, and since there was only one landing pad in that sector, Meeko sought to clarify his instruction, "don't use the observatory, Myk," he suggested and waited for the young man to reroute his course for the greenhouse before placing a video call to his mother. The scientist pulled up the 3D schematic of the facility from the hologram table. As he'd suspected, Meeko could see from the schematic the entire observatory was highlighted in red. The computer let him know Tee Wyr's last known log was still the observatory, so the techie was in there someplace. However, not only was his last known log the observatory, his last known execution code was clear for the scientist to see. Tee Wyr had killed off power. Deliberately.

Like every other call Meeko had made save his call to the observatory, the call to the infirmary didn't sail to video mail but went right through. He hadn't noticed that. When he came to notice that Lydia and Haku were on the end of it, chuckling, and trying not to expose too much Haku to the exposed video feed as he took a yellow syringe up his buttocks, Meeko didn't speak with a mind to mince words, "I can't reach Tee Wyr, Lydia. He's shut down the observatory."

"I don't think he would do that deliberately, Meeko. Maybe the power's out?" she responded as Haku adjusted his synthetic overall and joined Lydia by the video feed.

"No, he shut it down. With him inside."

"You are serious? That's quarantine protocol."

"What's quarantine protocol?" Haku asked but this was no time for questions.

"I want the two of you to meet me here at Centre. I'm initiating the bot to get you."

"Where's Myk?" Lydia demanded.

"No worries. I already told him to avoid the observatory. He'll be with you on your way back."

"What's happened to Tee Wyr? Where's my brother?"

"Hrth's outside the hatch with Pytrice. Like i said, you don't have to worry Haku. Just be here."

"okay," they terminated the feed, immediately on the move and leaving what was left of Haku's shots in a hurry.

****

They heard the thud from the hatch after they'd gotten in. Hrth came down the ladder first and Pytrice not long after he got off. There was this look on everyone's face besides Myk's. In sum, he was the only one with a smile on when Pytrice came off the ladder. She couldn't tell what was up with the made-up faces, but it was certain ol'pops didn't fancy what she'd done with his gravity scooter. Or going outside without a weapon in hand.

"What's up?" he asked uneasily because it appeared they'd been waiting for them.

"It's today," Haku announced pithily.

"I don't understand. What's today?" Hrth asked back.

"Today's the day you return home," Meeko answered on behalf of the four.

"You guys can't possibly be serious..." he muttered, but they looked serious enough. He sighed looking to Pytrice and how she would react to this stirring change, but Pytrice didn't want to show she'd been crying earlier so she hugged Hrth strongly and sped for the exit. Still not before giving Haku a tenuous hug goodbye and a very sublime kiss on the cheek. Everyone noticed the kiss and everyone after she'd sped out of there, looked to the elder brother—this little blonde was not the little blonde they were more than acquainted with. What did Hrth say to her? What did he do? No matter because all Hrth could do was shrug the questions away, refocusing on the matter at hand, "why today? That's absurd," he mentioned, redirecting his gaze at the grownups and trying to pick at the joke in all of this.

"Hrth! It's not a joke," Lydia said, trying to hide her obvious disconcertment with this new development.

"I thought you said we had a few more days, doctor? This is absurd," Hrth rejected strongly and Haku felt to concur. This was all too premature.

"We've already decided on this, Hrth. You have to go today," Meeko stated matter-of-factly, not really giving an opening for objection.

"Why? You really agree with this, doctor?" Hrth turned to Lydia, who was still holding up a made-up face and trying not to reveal the consternation behind it. "Obviously something's up. What's it?"

"It's the quarantine protocol. Tee Wyr's sealed himself inside the observatory, and no one knows what's wrong or why he's done it," Haku explained, wiping off any invisible traces of lip ink across his cheeks and trying not to blush at the memory of it.

"That doesn't mean we should leave? Can't we help or something?"

"Thank you, but we're long past that Hrth. The machines are already fired up for your journey back so now is the time to leave, unless you simply do not want to return home?" Meeko asked, but that was a rhetorical question. "You brothers are our future. You must remember that. Whatever happens here on out is no longer your concern. We'll be able to handle all this on our own," he admitted and for many obvious reasons

Hrth had no comeback to that. The old scientist fingered the brothers follow him to the INS Lab where the huge glass panes awaited, and locked behind them; a pair of Meeko's own time-displacement machines similar to Persephone in almost every way except for their simple glass covers.

coronal mass ejection

It was not until Myk locked down the transparent glass covers and sealed them in the contraption that Haku and Hrth truly realized this was going to be it. They were really doing this. Myk waved a mechanical goodbye on returning to the side of Lydia who despite her overzealous attempts not to show it, had been too frazzled to seal them in herself. Or say goodbye.

"What is this? What am I doing? What are we doing?" Hrth mumbled, venting his thoughts in the contraption for he could read her despondent face. What he hadn't realized was that this working contraption shared a biauditory connection with the other titanium contraption where Haku lay, and also with the main control room wherein Meeko worked both machines.

"Dr. Meeko says this is the right thing to protect the novel timeline. You heard him. This is what we should do," Haku replied and to Hrth's surprise. He turned to face his brother through the see-through glass.

"I know, but haven't you asked yourself why doesn't it feel that way? Does it feel like we are doing the right thing, Ruke?"

Haku turned his face away, probably in shame, "no," he admitted.

"exactly."

"but you know if we return we can save everyone—that's what Dr—"

"Maybe, but how can we expect to save everyone when we can't even save the people we know? You and Tee Wyr were close, weren't you?"

Haku didn't look comfortable. "Why are you using were?" he asked uneasily.

"Now powering up to twenty, Subject 1, Subject 2, Haku, Hrth, can you hear me?" Meeko cut into the connection, booming from somewhere inside both contraptions to uncouple their conversation. They nodded from within the contraption and he held up a generous and comforting smile to beguile them, but he wasn't fooling anyone. "Try to relax and control your breathing so this process isn't disorienting. I'm about initiating the countdown sequence," he announced to them, so the brothers waited for the countdown sequence to initiate, unknown to them Meeko had already kicked off the sequence. The old scientist had muted the audio countdown to allow the numbers run silently for he didn't want to rattle the brothers anymore than they already were on realizing they were having second thoughts. However, as they waited quiescently, Pytrice showed up beside Lydia and Myk. The brothers didn't expect the little blonde to show up from the get-go, but now? The fact that she'd be here to watch them leave? That was like a clarion call.

"This doesn't feel right. It feels like we're abandoning them," Hrth muttered on watching Pytrice hugging the plasma neurolizer like an invisible pet, almost in the same way she held on to the Balinese cat months ago. "No. We shouldn't leave this way," Hrth admitted uncomfortably.

"I don't know, Tagi," Haku said, sighing in guilt and equally frazzled by it. "You said before that this is beyond what we want. We'd be doing everyone a favour by leaving when we can. Unless we can have some sign from heaven of what's right and what's wrong."

"I think we should help them even if they don't want us to," Hrth concluded, hitting the play button by the side of this contraption, which months ago they hadn't realized was the eject button, and so the glass lid to his pod unhinged itself automatically.

"What are you doing?" almost everyone shot at him except Pytrice and Myk.

"You remain inside your pod, Haku," Meeko instructed sternly, and for the first time in their stay here the old scientist intended to threaten them. "Hrth return back to your pod!" Meeko announced, but deliberately didn't halt the countdown. Haku was the important one. He had less than 10 seconds to secure the future.

"You'll have to kill me because I'm not returning. Not today," Hrth said belligerently, planting his feet and looking to his brother behind the glass.

"Haku, you remain in your pod!" Meeko instructed but was half way out of the control room when Haku hit the play button and unhinged his glass lid.

"I'm not leaving without my brother," Haku stated as he exited his own pod just before the lightning struck in both pods.

"You recalcitrant wilful boys!" Meeko barked, grappling at his bleached hair in frustration as he approached them, truly upset, but both brothers held hands, and with it, a defiant smile.

"Recalcitrant wilful boys!" Myk parroted as everyone except Meeko and Myk had subtle smiles on their faces, and about the time the CME warning hit.

A recurring wailing sound commandeered the PA system and the power in the room waned ominously.

"You asked for a sign," Hrth said to Haku the same time as autistic Myk lost his temporal platitude. "CME! cMe! CME! cMe!" he warned over and over again when the red lights came on and all the equipment in the facility started to power down one by one.

"My god," Meeko panicked and raced for unit 15, followed by Myk, Pytrice, and Lydia after an almost inspiring look at the boys. The brothers ran to assist.

****

The five crawlers were on the walls when the warning sirens hit as Meeko resuscitated power to the observatory in anticipation of the cMe. Immediately, the crawlers were about the place, vigorously energetic, and reacting strongly to the whining. They punched through glass and amazingly shattered controls and levers, possibly in an attempt to stop the tenacious sound. Tee Wyr watched from within the glass compartment, not making a sound or any unusual gesture that could give out his location as these testicular crawlers, bigger and more muscled than the females, moved about erratically and belligerently in the observatory. In a few minutes, all the agitation will be over—that is if he survived the next few minutes, which lingered like a eternity, when one of the display screens in the glass compartment lit up. There was a lot of the static coming from the monitors, but the image was clear enough.

"Tee Wyr!" Meeko spoke from behind the comm. link and beneath the noise of the static, and continued to call, repeatedly, until the techie warily picked up the voice mail. Probably because Meeko's voice was getting too loud and would soon enough draw unneeded attention to the easy glass compartment he'd concealed himself in.

"Quiet down. I can't talk Meeko," Tee Wyr answered, lifting his head just high enough to keep an eye on the closest crawler to his hideout. The broad male was tearing at the control port and, for the lack of better words to describe what it was doing, studying the control port and its number of controls.

Meeko's face looked flushed, same as Lydia's who was standing next to him, "what's going on? Why did you lock down the observatory?"

"Are you sick?" Lydia interrupted having Haku share the screen with her. Or them.

"Hey! What's with you?" Haku queried, equally concerned and Tee Wyr almost managed a smile on noticing their blanched faces.

He huffed behind the comm. link. "Guys, I don't know how to put this but we have crawlers."

"What do you mean we have crawlers?" Meeko shot back from behind the comm. link. "You mean inside the facility?"

"this is my fault, it's the signals I sent in the mail. And I know you don't want to hear this now Meeko, but I want you to know i'm sorry. I'm sorry."

"You can be sorry later. What you need to do is get out of there!" Meeko advised, but Tee Wyr baulked at the suggestion on noticing a maned crawler heading his way, suddenly aware of this strange glass compartment. Or strangely finding its unbroken pane of glass curious. Or revealing so to speak.

"this is not a good time for me to talk Meeko. It's coming," he whispered back.

"Isn't there a way out?" Haku butt in when the wailing sounds stopped abruptly and Tee Wyr lifted the receiver to the cawing coming from behind the glass compartment.

"Can you hear that, guys? Stay there. There's no way out for me. All I hope for is they don't find me. I can't die this way. Not eaten by a crawler."

"You don't have a choice, Tee Wyr. That compartment's not shielded and we have a cMe coming in less than a minute," Meeko warned in a whisper. "You need to get to the cryo room. It's shielded. You just have to make a run for it. You have to go now."

"I have four of them here! I don't think i can make it before—" he'd started to say when crawler claws scratched against the glass panes, so Tee Wyr saw it sapient to kill the comm. link.

****

"Why don't we do something?!" Hrth suggested on the spur of the moment even as Lydia panicked, "boys! you need to do something!" So he requested the plasma neurolizer from Pytrice.

"What are you doing?" Meeko asked concernedly, but Hrth simply armed the neurolizer and headed out. "Where are you going Hrth?"

"You coming?" he said to Pytrice and immediately she followed.

"What are you two doing? Have you no cognitive function?" Meeko argued when the automated countdown sequence kicked in. They now had 25 seconds to seize whatever crazy plot they'd conceived in their mind to do.

"It's better than staying here and watch him get eating," Hrth rejoined and Lydia burst into tears because she just couldn't handle the tension.

"You know that's suicide? We're on shut down. You wouldn't be able to lift those doors because the power's down."

"i suggest you find a way to power up—" he answered obstinately when Haku butt in.

"I think i might know a way," he suggested only to meet with Meeko's asperity. The old scientist pointed two gnarled fingers at Haku's face, almost as if he wanted to hypnotise the early teenager, or poke his eyes out, "it's a definite no for you. You don't get any crazy ideas. You are staying put."

"I'm not going anywhere Dr. Meeko. You don't have to worry about me. Actually, no one has to go anywhere if this works," Haku spoke to all who were concerned and moved for the hologram table.

"What's on your mind?"

"His signals. Tee Wyr says they might work on crawlers."

"I thought you meant to get him out?"

"Yes, but no. Not like that. I'm thinking we can distract them—"

"So he can make a run for Cryo," Meeko finished off and jumped at the idea, finding it palatable as well as safe for all involved, "still that is if we can get to where he buried the signals," the old scientist muttered as he hit an override button on the hologram table and pulled up what looked like a jumbo of a gazillion files, "'cause the last time he went all techie on us trying to bring out those files."

They now had 20 seconds.

"Can't he do it?" Haku asked, referring to Myk who stood silently between Lydia's arm, persevering under the deluge of her tears.

"I believe he can," Meeko said and Lydia forcefully stopped crying.

"Myk," she had begun to whisper into his ears, but baulked and looked to Haku, "i need something to describe what it is we want him to search for? Myk's suggestive."

Haku didn't take too long in a muse to chime out the more than familiar rhyme, "everything dies that is not a sine function. Everything dies that is not a complex number, that's it!" he said, yet he'd barely finished the rhyme when Myk was at the hologram table, twisting icons and rewriting executable codes. He hit play before the automated countdown sequence hit ten seconds!

Although Meeko and Lydia didn't look surprised, Haku stood mesmerized by the boy wonder as the PA system automatically pealed out a sequence of noisy pulses. Hrth and Pytrice didn't need to go anywhere. "Why is it so loud?" he asked as they all put a hand to their ears because the pulses were almost deafening.

"I don't know, but I think it's better this way," Haku answered in a yell and in a way stopping Meeko from trimming down the volume.

"Why do you say that?" Lydia yelled.

"Tee Wyr says you say crawlers respond to sound," he answered and Lydia smiled, at the idea, despite her eyes and face been flushed from all the crying.

"I see your point. Thank you Haku."

"I just hope this works," Haku said as the countdown sequence hit 0 and like clockwork all the power in the entire facility went out and came back on after a silent number of seconds.

reanimation era

As with a general system's reboot, there was only static behind the comm. link when power rerouted itself through the observatory as every device came back online, including the display monitors.

"Tee Wyr?" Meeko spoke into the comm. link, trying to search out the screens for movement, or any sign of life. The observatory looked dishevelled, abandoned, and bare. "Tee Wyr are you there? Can you hear me?"

"Do you think he made it?" Haku asked, but Hrth wasn't up for guessing.

"It's been like—what?—2 minutes? There's no use waiting. Someone has to go," he announced, seeking to revivify the suspended rescue mission. Or was it suicide mission.

"I'm going with you," Meeko admitted.

"I'll come too," Lydia was forced to admit, wheedled by guilt. "He might be hurt," she said to justify coming along.

"Fine," Meeko accepted, but fingering at Pytrice to remain behind.

"Why?" the little blonde protested.

"Someone has to keep an eye on what's important," he instructed before turning to Haku, "if you do establish a connection before we get there, have him know we're on our way."

Haku nodded. "What about the crawlers?" he asked gravely.

"They are dead," Meeko answered matter-of-factly not revealing even a speck of concern.

"How can you be so sure?"

"it's safe," Hrth butt in, "I don't see them on the screen, do you?"

"No."

"Then we'll be fine."

"We'll be back. The observatory isn't shielded so there's no way they could have survived the cMe," Lydia chipped in to put Haku's heart at rest.

"okay. I'll continue here then."

"right," Meeko answered as the trio left for the observatory. The real mail button however had gone from green to red by the time Haku faced his new duty, so after a little poking around in futility, he looked to the little blonde with a sheepish smile, "er...I think I need a little help to work this thing?" he requested, but she just stared at him nonchalantly. He tried nudging her with the eyes but the little blonde shot him a scowl.

"What?"

****

There was still no response from the techie after she'd helped him unlock the giant computer.

"You could go. You don't have to stay here, you know? I can watch him," Haku said to her as she sat Myk on the sturdy hologram table.

"And who's going to sit here and watch you?" she mumbled back.

"for your information I can watch myself, but that's my point. It's never stopped you before. Just go. Do what you want to and don't pretend. Nobody likes a pretender," he said and his words bit into her.

"Who says I'm pretending?" Pytrice shot back, stuttering, and feeling stripped of all pride and power because she had no gun in hand. At any rate, Haku didn't have a rejoinder to that. Or maybe he did but decided to keep his words to himself. He turned his attention from her to face the monitors and could now see Meeko through one of the screens giving directions to Hrth and Lydia who were outside the screens; somewhere outside view. That was when he popped the question, without looking at her of course, "why did you kiss me?"

"What?"

It appeared she didn't hear him the first time, so he boldly repeated himself hoping not to get a thud from behind, "the last time. When you heard we were going home, you kissed me. Why?" Ruke could hear his heart beating, but the same way he could hear her breathe when she humphed. "Forget it," he hissed, knowing Pytrice and her steel vault for a heart. "I don't care or nothing, I only wanted to know because everyone saw it that's all," he let out in a disgruntled mumble, wiping off his chin with the back of his hand almost as if her kiss was somehow stapled to it.

"So what if I kissed you. It doesn't mean anything," she shot at him in what could have been statement or a question, he couldn't tell, but she obviously took offense at something.

Haku turned around to face his demon, "because everybody saw it. Even Myk," he said loudly and automatically autistic Myk got off the hologram table in response and came to him.

"and that makes it mean something?" she retorted.

"Read my lips. Yes. It means something because you kissed me but didn't kiss Hrth."

"What?" she asked again, almost as if she didn't understand him the last time.

He looked her in the eye, watching her pucker her lips at him, but tried hard to suppress an irate quiver, "you kissed Hrth but didn't kiss me!" he upended his words so this time she leered at him.

"You're doing it again!" he snapped.

"what am i doing?"

"go to the greenhouse if you need any help jogging your memory—"

"why would I want to jog my memory?"

"Arghh! Just go away," he quit haggling with her, but there was a smirk on Pytrice's face he couldn't wipe off.

"Hope you didn't like it. You didn't like it, did you?" she asked after a moment's peace of evading his questions.

He looked flushed, not deterred however, "who said—

stop these games and tell me why you kissed me?"

She chortled this time around. "So what? I did it to taunt you," she announced frigidly, hoping Haku would give it a rest, again feeling naked without a gun to point around.

"That's a lie," Haku snapped at the little blonde. He seemed angry with her. "It didn't feel like that and you know it."

"Why? What's it supposed to feel like?" she retorted, but he grew angrier. She could see it on his face.

"Why are you lying?"

"Who says I'm lying," Pytrice retorted, becoming all flustered and making up the distance between them. Actually, and on first thought, she had intended returning Myk to the hologram table, but now she shoved Haku to the ground to repress her anger. Or his questions. It was one or the other. "I only kissed you because my father said that's what a girl does when a boy likes her. He said my mother did, but now i know he lied too. It's not supposed to feel like anything because i didn't feel anything when I kissed you. Are you happy now?"

"That's another lie. You are a liar! And I hate you for it!" he yelled at her, rising almost immediately and charging at her like a wild bull. She dodged him effortlessly and Haku crashed into the hologram table, hurting his wrist or something close to it.

"You hate me?" she recited, irked, yet not knowing why

his saying that made her upset. "Now who's the liar? You don't hate me," she smirked, almost defensively.

"I do," he repeated and for another moment they exchanged frowns. This little battle wasn't quite over. She had to concede that he was taller and older than her so he charged at her a second time. This time around however, she decided against trying to evade him; to prove to herself not all boys are tough, and teach him not all girls are pushovers.

****

Every one of them was a big black blotch because being burnt out of existence was the power of a solar flare. As anticipated, there were four big black blotches against the metal flooring. They'd found one by the control port, one just outside the reactor room, one at the heart of the observatory, and one right inside the glass compartment. One more blotch and they would know the techie's fate.

"So this is what a CME does?" Hrth said wandering around the observatory as they searched it out.

"Yes. It kills off everything," Meeko answered all the way from his end of the perimeter search.

"I must have seen like a hundred cMe's, but I never anticipated this. Maybe bones, char or ash—but always thought it'd leave at least something."

"CME leaves nothing," Meeko answered, now picking up pace and heading for the cryo room, certain there were no more blotches in the huge observatory.

"What happens perchance this happens when we're outside?" he asked concernedly, "how have you survived so long?"

"It's easier to spot a CME from outside. We see the wall from miles away."

"You mean the wall of fire?"

"Yes."

"Boys, you mind?" Lydia injected when the three passed an utterly vandalized glass compartment. "What if he missed count? What if the crawlers got to him in Cryo?"

"I think we'll find that out soon enough. Is the neurolizer armed, Hrth?" Meeko requested and Hrth made sure. That was when they reached the rotating cylindrical door leading to Cryo, finding it sealed tightly. As they peered through its glass window, everything appeared to be in order. Astonishingly, there was also no trace of Tee Wyr but there were no signs they could see inside cryo either; nor did the frozen capsules appear to have endured any recent horror, but that when the techie slapped hard against the glass window from the inside. He'd been hiding behind the view of the glass all this while and was now jabbering through the glass.

Meeko placed his hand against the bioscanner and the door responded quickly, but not quick enough apparently because Tee Wyr grabbed at Meeko even before it fully opened up. "No! I said leave me in here," he said, not so sure if the three understood what he was saying to them as they all exchanged redundant glances in trying to make sense of the techie's state of mind. His rich hair all in disarray.

"How come?"

Tee Wyr noticed Hrth with the neurolizer. "Get him out of here! He can't be here! Or his brother."

"Haku saved your life," Meeko answered tersely, "but we're going to get them home today—"

"Then what are they still doing here? More are coming," Tee Wyr cut him short.

"You mean more crawlers?" Meeko stuttered apprehensively.

"Didn't you see it?" Tee Wyr demanded and Meeko looked to Lydia. "I put it up for you to see."

"See what?" the scientist retorted and suffice it to say he was more than confused.

"Weren't you listening? I sent it in the mail! It's what i've been trying telling you," Tee Wyr retorted, looking to the broken lenses above the observatory as if he was expecting something to come crashing through.

"We just had a CME. We were lucky we heard anything you said," Lydia cut in and Tee Wyr dashed furtively to the glass compartment looking ever at the lenses above for any sign of activity.

"When you say more are coming how many more?" Meeko asked uneasily, taking his cue from the techie's trepidation but Tee Wyr slapped in some control and execution codes before Meeko could ask why and immediately what appeared to be some kind of map popped across the little display screens. Pink dots dominated the outlay of it all. There were so many pink dots, and each almost as regular as small pox that Hrth felt quite uneasy about their number. Aside the fact, he somehow recognized the structure sitting at the centre of the map, if he recognized anything at all. It was the dome. "I piggybacked the signals. They know we're here.

"Are those crawlers?" Hrth asked uneasily.

"Every one of them," Meeko answered. "They planned this. Those were scouts. This isn't an accident."

"Isn't that saying they are already here?" Hrth asked on noticing a few pink spots bordering the outline of the map's dark concentric dome.

"But we just survived a CME?" Lydia argued.

"It's appears they did too. We're fools to think nothing's evolved since the reanimation era," Meeko muttered, his hand was already on Hrth motioning him for the hoverbot. "I think we've exhausted the minutes that last blast bought us. I need to get you out now."

"I blew it. None of you should have come for me," Tee Wyr said in despair, even as they dragged him along and made for the hoverbot.

"And how long did you think you could hold out holed up in there?" Meeko asked when more lenses shattered from high up in the dome and a wart-skinned well tanned brunette with prepubescent breasts hung from the metalwork. "No reckless movements," Meeko warned and they stilled all motion, with hearts in their mouths, as the creature monitored her environs closely. Somewhat pensively. She, or rather it, only screeched at them the moment Lydia powered the hoverbot. It hurled itself at them, away from the ceiling with such vicious force, that when Hrth fired the neurolizer he'd done so without any warning or concern for the others. The surprising thing, however, was that it didn't work, even if he'd fired it in the nick of time. They'd only escaped by the speed of the bot as Lydia had fallen on the throttle trying to hide her eyes before the neurolizer's blast of white light. The gun wasn't at fault. Deftly, the crawler had left its eyes closed. Then again, Lydia had evaded the creature's claws by the skin of her teeth without having realized it. It died from the unusual volt it got chasing the hoverbot into the massive electromagnet of the tunnels. They seldom had any moment to seal the blast doors after the bot, as it sped out of there.

"Shut down the observatory the moment we get to the other side," Meeko instructed, watching the crawler erupt in flames.

"I'd had it secured," Tee Wyr argued, quite upset they'd undone what he'd done. And done safely too, even as they heard more glass shatter from the observatory.

"I can believe these things were once like us?" Hrth muttered, disturbed by the sight, but in a way that could be mistaken for awe.

"Evolved, that's how they came about, Hrth," Meeko explained and the scientist rested a hand across the late teen's shoulder to pacify him, but Hrth jolted to his touch. Meeko no longer needed to prove a point. He could see it in the late teen's eyes. Now, more than ever, he was determined to leave this place. And all in one piece by the look on his face. "They are no longer like us, Hrth. These things are not people."

"H—How did it survive that blast?" he asked incredulously.

"They must have had shelter. Homo carnivarus anomalus survives by hibernating in the ground, or in some kind of rocky shelter—" Meeko had explained only for the biologist to usurp his explanation.

"Actually no one knows. That was the same thing our forerunners pondered when they encountered the first of these crawlers a long time ago in the reanimation era," she answered, shaken, and keeping her arms to herself, but barely able to keep a straight face, or her knees from knocking—a perfectly understandable reaction, the biologist having her own number of reasons why. "There was no food source that could support any multicellular creature out there. Nor did any plant life survive long enough after the blasts. Despite the odds, they still found them out there," she stated, and her voice quivered for saying it. "Nature doesn't always give us the answers, but it was no surprise they turned out to be meat eaters. These things."

"that wasn't what i had meant," Hrth replied.

"It doesn't matter what you meant. it's all the same," Lydia interjected weakly but Tee Wyr caught on very quickly.

"What he means to say is, we need to get the other guns if the neurolizer won't work," the techie announced, but that met Meeko's asperity because the scientist only had one place in mind Hrth was going— that was about the time the power in the tunnels waned.

"What this? Though now would be as good as any for another CME," he mentioned when the power waned again; this time a little longer, long enough for the bot to lose its suspension and make a violent dent in the tunnel.

"I don't think this is another CME," Lydia stated, wondering as with all of them what happened to the warning alarms and usual countdown heralding every cMe—when all of a sudden, the massive electromagnet failed completely and the bot made a dent so deep in the tunnel it threw them off. The bot didn't come back up. Neither did the power. But they hadn't wasted a second thinking about it, or the enveloping darkness, as they made a run for the terminal gateway using the only available light to lead them; the miniscule blue light emanating from the neurolizer.

It was fortunate albeit unfortunate on getting to the INS Center to discover the blast doors that should seal the tunnel remained open. All the doors were frozen in place actually, but after making their way through it wasn't so good a thing.

nest

On their way in they encountered them on their way out, which is why it didn't take long to sort out the oddities. "Why are you on foot? Where's the bot?" the little blonde and Haku demanded, on watching Hrth and the techie prop Meeko as they raced through the blast doors.

Meeko made his own demand immediately all three got off the channels and into the terminal gateway. "Shut the blast doors!"

"The schema's been flashing red a long time now, ol'pops. The doors wouldn't lock."

"that figures because the power's down in the channels," Tee Wyr mentioned.

"how come power's down in the channels?"

"the electromagnet—they must have short circuited it somehow."

"who's they?" she baulked.

"What we need to do is override those doors," Meeko stated.

"I don't how, ol'pops."

"Try the bioscanner. See if that works," Tee Wry chipped in, bearing so much urgency in his voice that the little blonde ignored getting answers and hurried for the blast doors.

"What's going on?" Haku asked immediately his brother

was close enough to hold.

"Crawlers," Hrth muttered gravely.

"Where's Myk?" Lydia demanded, on noticing the two without the third and Haku stuttered.

"We—we were one our way to find him."

"You lost him?" Lydia shrieked through her lungs.

"No. He was with us but..."

"Where is he?!"

"We don't know—"

"He's at the greenhouse," Pytrice answered after failing at the huge doors. The doors refused to shut.

"She thinks he's at the greenhouse," Haku rephrased, scowling and finding it easy to blame her instead.

"I know he's at the greenhouse, knucklehead. He's suggestive, but you just don't know how to keep your mouth shut," Pytrice argued.

Lydia lifted her hands for both of them to be quiet. She couldn't look at Pytrice, but when she did the little blonde looked away.

"How do you know he's at the greenhouse and not unit 5?" Tee Wyr questioned, "we have the bot."

"I'm just getting to know that, but we've already searched 5. He must have used the service hatch."

"but that's surface?" Meeko queried, grimacing, and leaving Lydia more in panic.

"I was going to get him," Pytrice replied in defence,

scowling at Haku. Perhaps wanting everyone to know whom to blame.

"No. We have crawlers. You remain here. I'll go get him," Tee Wyr butt in again. "And what's the passcode? I'll be needing those guns," he said as Meeko forced his limbs to stand on their own when he faced them.

"how could you? We trusted you—the two of you," he chided, but mostly his eyes were directed at the little blonde not Haku. Anyhow Tagho was there to glower at his brother.

"Watch the doors," Tee Wyr mentioned after she told him the passcode and Meeko turned to Hrth.

"Now that we agree you boys have satiated your superego, you need to leave," the scientist said strictly, as he made way for the INS Lab.

"That's fine. This time we're leaving," Hrth stated, aghast, and shoving the plasma neurolizer at Pytrice. But he looked more frazzled than he was upset with their deportment, so she turned away from him and looked to the channels. She didn't see any shadows inside the tunnel because all it lights were out in as much as it stood a wholesome black into the distance, but something seemed alive in there. The little blonde could tell. She could tell by just watching.

****

A storm was picking up because immediately Tee Wyr opened the hatch, the sands poured in. The gun in his hand wasn't at all like the neurolizer and had seen its share of dents and battle scars, but he wield it firmly, fastening the goggles in place as he launched himself out the facility into the rising sands outside. The winds and sand scratched at his goggles and gear immediately he was out into the near zero visibility of what was a sandstorm, and would soon be one with twisters for that matter. Yet he made his way with a simple gps device. When he was in proximity with the service hatch of the greenhouse, the device blipped and continued to blip until it remotely ran an executable code when he got to it. The service hatch mechanically lifted itself from the golden sands and Tee Wyr cautiously worked his way down the service ladder, draining a heaping mass of sand into the greenhouse for no one had used this surface hatch for years; they hadn't needed to for having the hoverbot running the underground channels sufficed. From the moment he climbed down, he tried not make a sound because he realized he wasn't the only one in the greenhouse. Many of the bouquets had been utterly damaged and the plants didn't seem at all their right number. Nor did the lights cast their usual cover. He armed the gun by pushing loose its safety cap and slinked across the first aisle he was closest to. There was valuable water and a burst bouquet across the floor, so he shut the breached faucet after finding it. Tee Wyr almost made it clear across the second aisle when he stepped into a fallen shrub, and it snapped. A loud enough snap to attract attention, that was sure. The techie turned around cautiously but saw nothing. Well since he saw nothing, he proceeded through to the next aisle. However, he had that indelible feeling he was being watched. Or followed. A feeling so strong he took unprompted glances over his shoulders and behind every now and then. When he scouted past the fourth aisle, he still hadn't found Myk, but with all the broken bouquets, the techie feared he shouldn't be here; but that was also when he stumbled into the glass splinter that nicked his foot. Now more than ever, he was sure he'd drawn attention to himself. Myk wasn't here. He'd thought better not to call, and in the middle of wondering why he had come here himself, and alone, when the techie smelt something foul. Or thought he smelled something foul. It seemed like the smell was building around him, so there and then, he decided to bail, retracing his steps to the service ladder—digitigrade. In the time he took him to come all this way, he'd never once looked up. This time, as he made his way back, Tee Wyr did. And there they were. Meat eaters coated in a sea of red against the ceiling. If this litter pool could be called baby crawlers, these were baby crawlers. Ten of them, male and female together! It struck him like an epiphany. It was the greenhouse gases. "It's a nest. They've come to nest," the techie couldn't help himself but mutter. Fortunately, much unlike matured crawlers, these critters were shy to the hunt which is why he'd made it this far, and also weren't reflex fast, so the techie got off a shot at the first crawler that launched for him. He shot it in the eye, which in using a projectile gun was the best luck that could happen to him. To tell the truth, it was the computerized projectile gun that had done all the work and sent the little crawler dropping in a simple thud to the ground. Suffice it to say, he had their attention, their full attention, as the litter pool came after him, including the crawler he had injured, so the techie took to the shadows, racing in circles and hoping to lure them away from the service ladder long enough before making his attempt at it when in the clear. One was already upon his thighs, but when the techie shot at it, the bullet not only ricocheted off its carbon reinforced skull but bounced dangerously around the greenhouse. He threw away the gun. He needed to be able look these things in the eye to best use it. Aside its weight wearying down his run. Or the oppressive heat from the greenhouse gases sneaking up on his consciousness, which at a time like this could end up more dangerous than how fast he needed to be to outrun these critters. He made his attempt for the service ladder in a one-time one-moment opportunity to get up and out of there, but just before grabbing the ladder something scratched him from a side, almost gorging his eye out, which was the reason he missed it; losing his balance and falling to a corner in the darkness. Immediately, the meat eaters gathered. All eleven and not ten of them!

It was also the moment the techie saw Myk, but then he bit his lip in regret, having already lost his gun. He hadn't anticipated grabbing Myk would be this much trouble, still he should have recognized beforehand the moment he perceived they were crawlers here and not overcompensate. What was it that got into him? What was it that got into his head that there was possibly more, possibly something, that he could do to atone for his mistake? This had all been his fault, but now also his downfall.

Myk, on the other hand, just sat in the corner watching the befuddling sight. He recognized the techie, yes, and in some way was waiting for something, something that wasn't forthcoming. So outside the screams and babble, he just remained there watching the crawlers eat the techie. However, not too long after, a low thud caught Myk's attention. There were curious prints against the half-opened blast doors, almost mathematical in outlay. Each blood print was a wiry hand, perfectly formed, and when he walked up the door itself, the prints seemed to rotate in a clockwise pattern, right up to the moment Myk looked through thee glass and saw them in scores—dead crawlers, that is, electrocuted against the huge electromagnet of a channel, but successfully shortcircuiting it, and witnessing live crawlers feeding off the dead crawlers like maggots in a feast. A number of these crawlers in the channels were drawn to the blast doors for some reason. They were drawn to Myk, but he was rarely animated behind the glass, so on sniffing him and getting a whiff of the baby crawlers he'd once had sniff him, the group left the autistic kid alone—returning to the channels, in the general run, for whatever was at the end of it.

****

"Someone needs to shut down the observatory," Lydia mentioned when she fell. A little blood was emanating from her side where she'd kept her arms firmly pressed.

Pytrice managed to keep her head from crashing into

the ground in the slow fall, "you're—she's bleeding!" the little blonde yelled for Meeko to hear where he was by the INS lab. Lydia was hurt and her temperature was up. Way up.

"Remind him to shut down the observatory," she said limply as a dark colour suffused the side of her breasts. Her face was pale and glazed, almost porcelain under illumination.

The little blonde found her lips quivering. "You're—"

"Remind him," she repeated, clutching Pytrice firmly by the hand, and again the little blonde yelled for Meeko, coming to note it was difficult for the biologist to speak.

"You're sick," Pytrice uttered.

"infected. That crawler we saw. Somehow it nicked me," she confessed very sickly, as the blood vessels by her arms protruded in darkened veins.

"Lydia's infected ol'pops!" Pytrice panicked as her hands quivered, and upon closer inspection noticed Lydia had more arterioles in the whites of her eyes than what anyone would deem normal. The pair would be bloodshot in a couple of hours if there was any truth to the stories. "She has crawler fever!"

"You should say something. You should always say something," the little blonde reprimanded her, biting hard on her lips after taking a look at the cut. It was a cut like any other cut, simple, even clean, but for the fact that it was killing her.

Lydia tried to laugh. Maybe lighten the little blonde's

concern by taking the scolding, but she couldn't. She hadn't the energy.

"I can go to 5. You have some needles there, don't you?"

She had to admit. Pytrice was no longer a child. "This is no ordinary bacterial infection."

"There must be something i can do, Lydia?"

"Tell Meeko to lock those doors," she reminded her.

"I know that already!" Pytrice yelled back angrily as she sobbed. "Tell me what to do. Lydia please!"

"Stay with Meeko. Stay alive," she mentioned, stroking Pytrice across the face and hoping to stroke away the fear imbuing her eyes, even as her motor functions began to wane.

"No! Stay! I want you to stay!" Pytrice demanded, hugging her tightly but Lydia's face was so white it frightened her. The doctor pet her blond hair limply. "No, fight. Fight it. I'll find Myk. I'll find Myk and bring him to you so fight it," she ground her teeth, clutching for straws and beating against Lydia's breasts which strangely felt firm. Or harder—bouncier so to speak. "You have to fight it. Fight it Lydia!"

"Myk," the biologist muttered, despair in her voice as the infection spread to her lips having worked its way around her lymphatic system, and now eating through her nervous system, soon to set in full body paralysis after a not so detailed number of seconds.

"Help ol'pops! Ol' pops please!" Pytrice yelled and

somehow she thought she heard Meeko call back. "I'll get those shots. I'll get you the whole thing!" she said, about leaving when she heard a loud thump from the down the tunnel. The little blonde couldn't shear her eyes of its harrowing blackness. If what was coming was the crawler that nicked Lydia, this one had the sickness too.

****

"Get in!" the old scientist instructed when he heard Pytrice call for his attention.

"I think i hear Pytrice?" Haku asked first, still in the process of getting his pod open when a little blood trickled from a corner of his mouth. Fortunately Hrth was already inside his pod.

"What happened to you?" Meeko asked, hinting at Haku's cheek.

"oh it's nothing," Haku replied ruefully, wiping the streak off his cheek.

"Inside now," the scientist instructed inflexibly.

"Isn't that Pytrice?" Hrth asked and for the second time the old scientist could hear her groaning for aid in the distance over the humming of the pods, nevertheless he coffined both brothers in the contraption. In fact, once he'd secured both lids, Meeko proceeded for the control port, running both numbers and countdown with animated precision. "Reinitiating the countdown from 10," he announced to them from inside the control centre. "Remember what i told you. Try and stay still, and control your breathing, the two of you, so you don't feel queasy—" he said around the time the power went out, plunging the entire INS in sudden black out.

"No. Not the reactors. Not the reactors," Meeko prayed to himself, providentially the blinding lightning that followed seconds after didn't come from the reactors. Or the pods. No. The conspicuous and continuous flashes of lightning lighting up the INS was emanating from the neurolizer. It was Pytrice. It seemed the little blonde was in more trouble than he'd thought.

desolatus

The moment the lights went out, Haku was suddenly at a war with the glass lid. He wasn't sure what to do or if Meeko, or his brother, could hear him from inside the contraption. He needed to get out of the glass coffin even if it meant he had to hurt himself to get out. However the next time he attempted kicking the glass, he kicked Hrth.

"Quiet. Quiet! Stop struggling," Hrth mentioned when he lifted the lid off its hinge. And without the proper words to explain it, the early teen felt a burden lifted off his breasts. He could breathe now.

"Hrth! What's going on? I can't see you," Haku panicked, groping for his brother in the dark until three middle fingers stumbled into Hrth's face.

"Watch it. You don't want to poke my eyes out."

"Sorry. What's going on?" he asked again, lowering his voice to a whisper.

"The power's out. It's just like when we were in the tunnel. Something's gone wrong," Hrth whispered back, securing his arms around his brother and lifting him off the contraption.

"Where are we going?"

"Meeko isn't back. We need to get out of here."

"Where?"

"Rukewe, I don't know. Let's find Meeko first," he

answered and they raced, hand in hand, away from the pods, but that was when flashes illuminated the INS in shades of light. Hrth recognized the neurolizer and immediately headed the wrong way.

"But Meeko's the other way? We are we going?"

"Just stay behind me," the older brother susurrated, using the flashes of light as stepping stones to someplace, but that was when they saw it in the distance; the first of many that had made it through the blast. And then another, and then the next, creeping along the walls like an army of ants. A host of devils.

Haku pointed but Hrth seized his hand, "no reckless movements," he warned.

"is that..." Haku muttered.

"Yes."

"Holy Horus. Are we going to die?"

"Not if we step back."

"now?"

"Yes. Do it slowly and quietly," Hrth instructed in less than a whisper, but it was already too late. In fact, his whispers were more than enough to attract their attention.

****

With no power, the entire INS was pitch-black, so before he could make his way to the pods, Meeko needed a lithium flashlight. By the time he could find one and return to the INS Lab, somebody or something was already in with pods. Meeko flashed his light around but when he heard cawing from the walls went as still as a stillborn pup. The pods already had their lids up. The boys were out. Or had been taken, he'd thought, when a hand grappled him by the shoulder. "You're alright..." he sighed when he mechanically cast the light against her.

Pytrice fingered and pointed at something creeping in slowly, from outside the protective glass. They were on the walls, progressing quickly and stealthily like roaches to wherever they felt drawn. Her eyes were sore and red. The old scientist fell on his knees and grabbed the little blonde by the waist clutching her tightly.

"I see them. Where's Lydia?" he asked into her ears, relieving the hug and looking into her eyes with the lithium flashlight each time he spoke. The little blonde shook her head. "They have her?" he inferred beneath a whisper and she shook her head again solemnly, without as much as a sob. "Poisoned?" he barely uttered, and by poisoned he'd meant crawler fever so she nodded, struggling not to accrue tears. He hugged her dearly this time, swallowing down hard.

After a long pause, he muttered, "where you able to do it?" but this time a tear rolled down her cheek for in advent of such a complication, it was their duty to keep anyone from being eaten—in any euthanatized way possible. He pecked her upon the neck. "If she's paralyzed, she won't feel anything. You did well, petridish. It doesn't matter," he assured the little blonde, but saying that only made Pytrice whimper. He locked her lips, and in the nick of time too, when he noticed a few shadows outside responding to her sobs.

"Where are the brothers? Where's Haku?" he asked into her ears, so decidedly she wiped off her tears against his hair before turning Meeko's lithium flashlight to the right. And there the brothers were, outside the glass, surrounded and alone.

****

In a way every craawler could see them, before and after both boys ran a corner. That was until they hit a wall. Or something equally as hard. Now, there was nowhere else to run so Hrth stood still in the darkness, holding tightly to Haku, and in his way keeping him from groping in the dark. If in any way they were cornered, they were to remain still and mute. And so they did even when they almost lost their teeth by bumping into the wall. But now, there was this awful stink around them, all too malodorous to describe—not a stink stemming from decay, yet presumably from the meat eaters, which was about the time Meeko's lithium flashlight cut through the darkness and Haku could see the shadows that for a while had them running in blindness. These blanched complexioned beasts, allegedly once humans, literally hung from the walls, sniffing the air and moving around stealthily. It seemed, in their stillness, these creatures had lost track of them, walking on all fours like big apes; a number of them wandering haplessly past them, but none reacting to the very intense lithium flashlight coming from no place other than the INS Lab. At least, help was somewhere across the light. But how to get from here to there without being torn apart by these meat eaters was the puzzle.

Haku stared at the light source expectantly, yet as anticipated by Hrth, Meeko's flashlight didn't move an inch. Nothing was moving around the INS that wasn't a crawler. Nothing could afford to move around the INS that wasn't another crawler. Apparently, they were stuck. With no assistance forthcoming Haku looked to Hrth, knocking his head towards the light and implying they make a run for it, but Hrth's bold irises stared at him fiercely, dark and glazed over. He squeezed Haku by the fingers almost till it hurt. It was his way of saying no. A stern no. No one expected the crawlers to be this many. Not even after the number of pink dots he'd seen barely an hour ago. Next thing they knew, a grating sound came scraping against the titanium flooring, making its way from across the place of light towards them. The brothers stared in horror as the gravely unwanted attention slid to Hrth's foot—armed to full damage and ready to fire. It was Pytrice sending them the plasma neurolizer, but now every crawler wandering about in the INS momentarily became mindful of the two brothers.

"Close your eyes!" Hrth cautioned as he reached for the neurolizer, shooting his first pulse without a second warning. This time, not to exaggerate, all the crawlers fell lifeless beneath its pulse. Hrth grabbed Haku almost immediately. "Are you okay? Are you alright?" he demanded impulsively, but it was near impossible for the littler one to shear his older brother off despite the fact that he was all right.

"I'm okay," he replied when the light bounced in their direction. The voice behind it was a familiar one. Hrth examined him sketchily. So did Meeko.

"is he okay? If he's okay, we need to get to the hatch," Meeko instructed even as Pytrice yanked the neurolizer from Hrth, not taking even a moment to receive his gratitude. She had two fuel cells with her and without ado, swopped one cell for the cell arming the titanium gun.

There was movement in the darkness. One of the crawlers was still breathing. In fact all the crawlers were still breathing. Or twitching. Haku inched over to examine them sketchily.

"They aren't dead," Haku mentioned and motioned to poke one by the loin to feel if what it had on was flesh, proving the tales true, but Meeko tugged him towards unit 5. "I thought they were dead?I"he mentioned. The breathing crawler felt as hard as muscle.

"Where's Lydia?" Hrth asked the little blonde but Meeko tugged on Hrth too.

"In a minute, crawlers will overwhelm this place. We need to get him to the hatch," he cautioned and they raced for the hatch.

"I thought Lydia was with you?" Hrth asked Pytrice again under his breath, but the sore look in her eyes told him more than he was jousting for.

"Where's everyone?" Haku asked on getting to the

ladder but knowing the kid was fine, Meeko gave Pytrice the eye, now commuting to eye talk, so she handed her neurolizer to Hrth, mounting the ladder readily to manually unhinge the hatch.

"You just have to worry about getting home, Haku," Meeko responded dryly helping or securing Haku up the ladder after Pytrice.

"But where is everyone?" he asked as the little blonde opened the hatch and sand poured in from the storm outside.

"Watch your eyes," she admonished.

"I've said this a thousand times. Keep your mind on getting home. You have to get home, Haku," Meeko said from below, watching Haku and Pytrice exit the facility but keeping Hrth from getting on the ladder. "Hrth, I'll have to ask of you the heaviest of prices," he confessed in less than a whisper and Hrth stood dumbfounded. In truth, there was nothing to say.

****

On stepping outside, the storm was in full rage. The sands had blot out half of the sunlight and there was a lot of funny lightning, yet nothing that could take away that funny tingling inside Haku that something wasn't right. The moment Pytrice shut the hatch on everyone else however, he knew something was up.

"You shut it!" He protested, but there was the sore look of indifference in her eyes.

"Watch your eyes. Watch your mouth," she muttered,

standing over the hatch as sand whirled about them, tearing at their arms plus everything exposed and drawing blood.

"Why did you shut it?" Haku asked, already in panic aside from the incessant lightning searing through the desert. This time there was thundering and Haku ducked his head in response.

"ol'pops says so," she confessed bluntly, not in the mood to apologise for it.

"What about my brother?!" he yelled, scrambling for the hatch but finding it dead. Or without power. Still she shoved him off. "You locked him inside!! There are crawlers in there!!" he announced, keeping his voice above the thunder.

"Meeko says to get you home," she retorted, revealing the second fuel cell in her hand.

"I'm not leaving without my brother."

"You're going. Don't make me make you," she grumbled under the winds but he didn't look daunted by her sore eyes—his was also one of emotion.

"Open it Pytrice!" Haku said and it was the first time he said her name out loud.

She didn't care what he said.

"Open the hatch," he said, sterner than the first time and forming his fists into a ball. It appeared he hadn't learnt his lesson their last fight, so she stood there, watching him throw a fit.

"You act like Meeko never told you anything of what the

prophecy says," she said succinctly.

"I know what the prophecy says—it doesn't say i can leave without my brother!" he yelled angrily and she realized all this while ol'pops never said anything. Still, she washed the expression off her face. Ol'pops must have had his reasons.

"Why do you think ol'pops calls you the important one?" she muttered and he lost his voice, or vigour because when he shoved her by the shoulders to get her out his way, it was a gentle shove. Hardly one to start a fight.

"Open the hatch!"

"No."

"You locked it! Open it," he wrestled, locking hands with her.

"No," she retorted, her eyes a fiery pink standing in pale contrast to her ashen lips.

"I'm not going anywhere without my brother," he stated, with a foot down and two soft brown irises reflecting back her tenacity.

"You are!"

"You can't stop me," he retorted, attempting to slip his arms past her but she got to his shoulders first. This time though, much like the last time, she took him wholly by surprise by kissing him when he tried wriggling her into an arm lock.

There was no sound but the lightning, thunder, and storm raging around them. They felt nothing, nothing except the kiss, and pure adrenaline coursing through their young veins.

****

"I promised to get you both home safely and i will, but the INS control centre is the only place i can program the time displacement machines outside to send you boys home."

"But how are you going to do that? There's no power in the INS," Hrth asked doubtfully, for it was obvious they would still be in darkness without the help of the lithium flashlight.

"The board at the control centre is wired to go a week without power. We just need to get to it. This power outage is only in the INS, that's why i need you. Those machines outside are not going to work without marching orders."

Hrth looked at the hatch forlornly before agreeing. It was dangerous, yes—possibly reckless, yes, but his hands were tied.

"But what about crawlers? What about leaving them alone up there?" Hrth demanded, needing to know why the scientist would go kamikaze with their lives, or if this was indeed his last straw.

"There's a storm up there. Crawlers don't come out in storms. They'll be fine," he responded.

"That's what you said the last time," Hrth rebutted and Meeko saw the point.

"What can i say? They have each other, just like we have each other. It's the crawlers nesting in here you should be worried about. Can't say that gun worked for all of them. We better get moving. Some might wake up, but more are coming," he said and Hrth got his point. They focused the flashlight against anything that moved in the dark, but aside the crawlers suffering from severe convulsions there was hardly anything moving in their immediate vicinity. They did a good job to keep from stumbling or falling over stuff in the dark, Meeko made sure of that, but that was still they got to the control centre and Meeko powered up the hologram table. When its green light powered up revealing incidental schemas of the facility; sectors that were faulty, powered down or disabled, and the two time-displacement machines outside currently on shut down, Meeko actuated the time displacement sequence, running all the numbers and transferring all initiations to port two, the older of the machines outside, yet that wasn't all Meeko initiated for the old scientist had spotted movement in the shadows.

"There," he pointed and Hrth blasted off the neurolizer. "There," he pointed again and again, but with every shot, more crawlers seem to animate in the darkness.

"I didn't expect them to be this many," Hrth announced.

"That's what they do when they nest. They are drawn together. We learned that ad desolatus. We might have to use that cell in your pocket. You have the cell?"

"Yes. Pytrice handed me the fuel cell."

"Uncase it and hand it to me."

"I'm kind of busy Meeko," Hrth retorted, speaking with

his eyes firmly closed and firing another pulse.

"Then give me the gun. You'll have to expose the case and strike it against the titanium till it glows red," he said, both men keeping their eyes firmly closed for each pulse.

When Hrth tried to hand over the gun, he found he couldn't do it in time before letting off another pulse at yet another wave of crawlers. Truth is, the hologram table might have been a useful tool designed for running executable codes and tracing programs but not avoiding crawlers because it was every byte as loud to crawlers as the tinkering it made when running those programs. "What happens when it glows red?" Hrth asked but the old scientist didn't answer. "Meeko, what happens when it glows red?" he asked again, keeping his eyes open this time and looking to Meeko, but Meeko was gone; simply gone, or dragged away in a ligature of his own blood, for there was blood leading into the darkness around him, blood that wasn't there when they first came in. No one expected them to be this many. Just as no one expected him to watch the corners, either. The INS control centre was counterproductive; Hrth hadn't recognized earlier it had much equipment that could shield things from the neurolizer's blinding light. So many corners that not even the neurolizer could save him from a grave fate if he didn't make a run for it. Hrth stripped open the fuel cell and slapped it against the ground first—so hard it turned magenta before glowing red.

****

There was a slight boom underground; even Pytrice felt it, so Haku fearing the worst, popped out of the time displacement pod in the same manner the machines had popped out of the sand earlier, betraying the last few minutes the little blonde had invested chicaning and misdirecting the younger brother to get into the pod.

"Pretend you didn't feel that," she yelled to him from behind the contraption, trying to keep her bleeding hands steady while fixing the fuel cell into Haku's pod. It came as a bit of surprise to watch its active light go on. Ol'pops had already sent in the coordinates. He had done it.

"I can't."

"I told you—"

"I know what you told me, but i can't. I can't just take your word for it."

"You're so stubborn. You don't listen. You're going to die if you don't listen," she snarled as the pod actuated a steady humming.

"I can't leave without my brother! I have to go help them," Haku said, running off, his arms and feet used to bleeding out from the whirring sands. A little more of Ra and Horus were out now, their rays erratic through the twisters.

"Stay! We can't go back!" Pytrice yelled, racing after him, only having twenty seconds to get him into the pod now that she'd inserted its fuel cell, but as ol'pops had promised they found Hrth heading their way through the sands.

The brothers locked in embrace even as the sands tore at them.

"You're alright! You're alright!"

"I'm fine."

"She said was i to leave first, that you were coming but i couldn't go. Not without you."

"You should have. There was something Meeko and I had to do, but we can't keep risking everything like this. Even for me."

"at least you're here. Where's—"

Pytrice yanked him by the shoulder. "Your pod! It's started!" she yelled and they ran to it. When Haku divided into it, there was concern in his eye, "are you coming with us? Is she coming with us?" he asked before either Hrth or Pytrice could close the ground glass.

Hrth shook his head. "Pytrice wasn't born in our time. I don't think she wouldn't make it if she comes with us, Ruke. She'll die," Hrth pleaded.

"No!" he refused, more than concerned, and carelessly letting grains of sand into his eyes to show it.

The little blonde took him by the jaw and kissed him full in the mouth before he could scratch his eyes out. This time, unlike the last time, she didn't kiss him under pretences to get him move along. This time, just like the first time, it was a warm kiss and he felt it in her kiss. Hrth chose not to interrupt them even though the clock was ticking.

"I told you to watch your eyes!" she growled at him, shoving him back into the pod with tears pooling in her eyes when Hrth sealed the chamber, and just in time for the lightning to start.

"But why do you have to die! Why does anyone have to die! that's not fair!" Ruke cried rapping against the ground glass even if they couldn't hear him, but Hrth wouldn't raise the ground glass.

The lightning came and took Haku away in the twinkling of an eye. Hrth raised the ground glass just to be sure nothing remained.

"Where's Meeko?" Pytrice asked when Haku was gone but this time Hrth was the one with sore eyes. She hugged him tightly, so tight he could hardly let her go.

"Do you want us to attempt it?"

"I can't," she sobbed, letting him go and taking the neurolizer from him. "It's your turn," she said on spotting static numbers reset themselves and a green light flashing concurrently inside the pod.

"Are you going to be alright?"

"You have 20 seconds, just go! I can look out for myself. I'll find Tee Wyr," she said and Hrth held her pale little hands tightly, so tightly he kissed them before he manoeuvred his way into the contraption.

"Thank you," he said in parting, "now I understand why Meeko is so adamant this is not a time machine. This place, this time we share and call the future is actually our past because it doesn't change that we were here, with you, that we lived, with you, that i got the chance to share my life, with you, and Meeko, and—"

Pytrice didn't want Hrth to see her cry, or give more ear to his sentimental ear-licking, so she closed the ground glass on him. He could only chuckle through the water gathering in his eyes, being it her way, but not before spotting something moving stealthily or swiftly from behind the storm. And as it happens with water pooling in his eyes, the late teen didn't give it much thought because the storm was strong. However, the lightning he caught from inside the ground glass didn't come from the pod—it came from the neurolizer as Pytrice tried to defend herself and Hrth's pod last minute from a crawler before the green light flashed the twentieth time. And it did. It did flash green the twentieth time, but only after the crawler smashed through the ground glass and ripped its contents open. It was a maned male, this one.

time displacement

Travelling through space and time is more nerve-racking than sailing through a magnificent portal of colours and light. What it feels like, what it really feels like, is an immediate and all engulfing experience of the senses; the retina hurts as the optic nerve is befuddled by a sudden jolt of new light, the middle ear sustains an echo from the strain of two worlds, the ionized air inside the small chamber fills with particulate carbon and tastes like metal in the mouth. Actually, the entire body takes an acute awareness of itself—right down to the very last blood vessel! A strange thing. It's almost as if the brain for a few seconds automatically takes a roll call of everything present and anything missing. If missing.

In the twinkling of an eye, Haku found himself banging against the ground glass where the sky looked much different through the glass. Hrth and Pytrice were hardly gone from view when Haku hit the play button beside the chamber and the ground glass popped open on one hinge. It opened up and he took a moment to collect his thoughts. He had a clear view of moisture laden clouds and the sun the way he'd always known it—a single sun towering brilliantly over a citywide skyline.

"Halloo! Who's there?" a voice called from somewhere away and he could hear flurried footsteps approaching. When he motioned to get out of the pod however, what Meeko had feared came true. Haku couldn't keep a retch down and puked all over the chamber just after staggering out of the pod. He stood speechlessly. Hrth would be so pissed because he'd be arriving soon. With a little luck, maybe he'd arrive in the next chamber.

"yes! who you?" the voice asked from a pile of four or five cars down and so the early teen realized he'd was atop a giant Mack truck. He was back, at Orido's gunky work garage, and this much older boy with tucked sleeves who questioned him was most certainly one of his apprentices.

"Er..i?" Haku couldn't explain what he was doing up there. Neither could he explain why he mulishly remained by the titanium time-displacement pod.

"Er..er...what? I asked who are you? And why are you there?" the work boy demanded, sounding terse this time; an eye of askance about him as he sized up the potential pilferer.

"I'm waiting for someone."

"Who?" he asked warily, looking left and then right but finding no one else in the work garage.

"M—my brother. I'm waiting for m—my brother," Haku answered, and in a drawn stutter because Hrth should have arrived by now; Hrth's sudden coming might even explain his awkward reticence to the stranger below.

"So where's this brother?" he barked back, now upset the little thief had no plausible excuse.

"I—I—I know uncle Orido," Haku stuttered in defence because it was now almost impossible for him to arrange his thoughts. Where was Hrth? Where was

Tagho? Didn't he make it? Or was the machine not working?

"Aah ha! For your information, this is my dad's work garage. I know everyone he knows and I don't know you," the work boy retorted after gaping, folding his arms and waiting for the liar to come down.

"Tell him Aunt Roseline sent me," Haku said and the look across the work boy's face was one of severity not acknowledgment.

"Wait there," he growled and took off with this look on his face. Most likely to go get his father.

Haku reached for the ground glass lid, hoping if he returned the lid to its proper position, Hrth might magically appear, but then he had so little space atop the broken down Mack to stretch himself so far that the titanium machine buckled to the weight of the lid and fell off the Mack in such a big loud bang that it splintered the glass in the pod to bits. "Hrt—Tagho! Tagho! Why isn't he coming?" Haku cried when the work boy returned on his heels, drawn to the noise.

"He broke it! He broke the glass! Weren't you going to fix that!" the work boy announced when he return with a rough hewn man. "Even if you repair it, you can't sell it with the lid gone."

"Who are you? Why are you destroying what's in my workshop?" the man boomed at Haku, but if truth be told it kind of was hard to tell to whom he referring.

"Er—you're not uncle Orido. I don't know you," Haku

stated, sore-eyed.

"Uncle? I don't know you," the man retorted, contorting his face in askance.

"He says he knows Roseline. I thought you had nothing to do with her anymore, Pa."

"Shut up! I don't," the alleged Orido shoved his son across the head. "You! Come down here."

"I can't. My brother—"

"Is there anyone else here stealing in my garage?"

"He's been saying that all morning, but there's no one here. There's no brother, Pa."

"Go see!" Orido shoved his son to look around the garage. "It's not enough that i have one thief in my garage, but two?"

There was something about theft that didn't sit well with Haku. He was down before Orido was done talking and racing for the gate before either the mechanic or the mechanic's son could grab a crowbar and give chase.

****

He'd spent more than a week at the NISD, and though the early teen had been dreading this phone call in addition to today's meeting, or interview as the men at the NISD see it, he was obligated to. Asides, the men of the National Institute of Science and Development rarely saw any activity, so this meeting wasn't only going to be the highlight of their year but would serve as a ticket for their carriers.

"They're here. Are you ready?" a man he'd come to know as Enosa asked quite excitedly. Enosa had been smoking but he quickly killed it; his ebony lips and hands trembling from the adrenaline. "There they are," he said as a round burly man, an ebony man, almost one the early teen thought he'd seen before, came through the glass doors leading a delegate of multinationals—Africans, Americans, Europeans, and Orientals. They waltzed into the single storey building as if they owned the place. The easy going of the lot were smokers. Others stiffer than a stick. Even a few looked grim. Grim from busyness. Or grim from fatigue.

The burly man walked boldly to where they were with doubtful, or rather scrutinizing eyes, "so this is the young mind that solved the unitary equation?"

"Yes sir. He is the one. We now call it the Meeko equation—at his request," Enosa said with a smarmy smile as the others in the burly man's company looked pensively at the early teen.

"How old are you?" he demanded brusquely.

"four—teen," Ruke stuttered and Enosa quivered into the dialogue.

"As you can see he is as we described two weeks ago."

"That remains to be seen," the burly man said and despite the rather unpredictable expression he wore, warmly offered the early teen a hand. "It's a pleasure," he announced pithily.

Ruke took the hand, but lost his voice instead, "thank

you, sir," he sort of replied, slightly pertrified and barely able to mutter.

The burly man turned to Enosa, "the minister informs me you have a story to tell us? These are very important people," he emphasized and with good reason because he hadn't the time to rush into introductions over each man in the delegate of multinationals behind him. "He went through a lot of trouble getting them here."

"Yes, but i must confess it is his story. This little man has something quite important to say. I know you will all find what he has to share interesting, which is why the minister himself arranged this meeting."

"Very well then," the burly man said and led the delegate to a conference room with see-through glass walls, a projector sitting on the oblong table, an interactive white board, and over a dozen seats neatly arranged with the appropriate tablature for the delegate.

Enosa looked at Ruke feverishly, "you asked for this. I believed you and arranged this because you've already solved what we thought was a near impossible equation from where Einstein left off. That man, the one who took your hand, is the regional director of WHO, and those men, the ones following him, some are from NASA and the World Bank. These men have the resources to change the world, and though this is frightening, you have to tell them the truth there. The whole truth. Leave nothing out of it, okay?" he demanded and Ruke nodded slowly, but before the early teen could motion for the hallowed office, Enosa placed a cell phone in his way. "Are you forgetting something? I'd advise you otherwise. The machine is still in the garage. We've cleared the area but we thought better not to touch anything. Your brother still hasn't come through though, which brings me to the other reason why I'm doing this. This is a photo of you taken yesterday," he said handing over a high resolution photo of Ruke, in the company of his father and brother with slouched faces, exiting a football viewing centre. It felt like three months ago. "The other you i mean. We found your home. I traced the address you gave me. That's you in the photo, isn't it?" he asked, but intending it to be a rhetorical question. Ruke could only take in a breath at the living picture of himself and the flood of memories that came pouring in.

Enosa sighed. "This is big. Two yous. We're going to stun them in there, which is why I'm not sure about this. Are you sure about this? Do you want to do this? I mean really do this?" he asked, handing over the cell phone. "I mean talk to your family?—they might not understand."

Ruke nodded simply, too stunned to talk.

"Okay. I'll go start but you'll have two minutes to join us?"

Ruke nodded again so Enosa left him there with cell phone in hand to go begin the meeting. Ruke dialled the eleven digit telephone number already waiting across the screen but when it rang, with each tone it rang, his heart virtually skipped a beat.

"Hello? Hello?" a voice asked through the cell phone, and for a moment Ruke couldn't recognize the sound of his own voice. He kept wondering in silence who was speaking when someone else yanked the phone, cautioning the little rascal not to pick up dad's cell phone without permission. Immediately Ruke recognized Hrth's voice, despite all the rowdy traffic and the noisy roar of local thugs around that vicinity. He found his voice.

"Who's this? Our dad's driving. You want to leave a message or call back?" Tagho asked even as tears welled up in Ruke's eyes.

"I really miss you," Ruke mentioned, his voice cracking up, not having intended to cry. He cleared his throat to sound better and not disconcerting, but Tagho totally misread what he said.

"it's a real issue?" the late teen asked back yet without a second thought passed on the phone to the man behind the wheels.

"Who's this? I'm driving," a raspy but very familiar voice answered next, and for another long moment Ruke could barely summon the courage to answer. "I said who is this?!" he demanded.

"I miss you dad! Can i come home? I want to come and see you? I want to see Hrt—no, Tagho. I just miss you all so much i had to call," Ruke requested, but the raspy voice grew terse.

"Who? What are you talking about? Listen mister, you must have the wrong number!" his father had barely answered, thoroughly upset, when Ruke heard the accident for a second time in a row. To be frank, its ear-splitting sound was hard to miss.

You can add to your library of
phantom house books.

GENERAL FICTION

THE BEDSIDE AND CAMP FIRE SERIES

Request for your favorite titles and our
newer books at your local bookshop or
visit your online retail bookstore.